Good Advice for Bad People

For

Bad People

The Collected Advice Columns of 

Vol. 2

PATRICK THOMAS

PADWOLF PUBLISHING INC.
WWW.PADWOLF.COM
www.facebook.com/Padwolf

WWW.PATTHOMAS.NET
WWW.DEARCTHULHU.COM
www.facebook.com/PatrickThomasAuthor
I_PatrickThomas @ Twitter

Dear Cthulhu,

I'm in a real pickle of a problem. Recently I went out drinking with my cousins, to the point where I blacked out. I woke up in my aunt's barn, naked except for a torn condom. I was cuddled up with a sheep. I live in a very religious community where this would be frowned upon. I would probably be ostracized and even made fun of.

My cousins think it's hilarious. They call me a dumb hick and even told me that the sheep was in heat and is now in a family way. I mean a human can't impregnate a sheep, right? I kind of think nothing happened and they set up the whole thing, but how can I be sure? I'm too embarrassed to ask my folks. Can you help me?

    -Asking Ewe for Help

Dear Ewe,

I have sad news for you, being as naive... or rather as concerned as you are. Humans can indeed cross breed with sheep. The spawn look like satyrs. Your cousins did nothing. You should have kept it in your pants. Now you have to deal with the consequences. Since you claim a religious upbringing, you have only one choice. Do the right thing and marry the sheep. Do you know how much hay and oats a sheep and litter of satyrs eat every day? And that doesn't come cheap, so you better drop out of school to get a job to support your new family.

***DEAR CTHULHU*™ Series**
HAVE A DARK DAY - GOOD ADVICE FOR BAD PEOPLE
CTHULHU KNOWS BEST - WHAT WOULD CTHULHU DO?
CTHULHU HAPPENS - CTHULHU EXPLAINS IT ALL

***THE MURPHY'S LORE*™ SERIES**
TALES FROM BULFINCHE'S PUB
FOOLS' DAY: *A Tale From Bulfinche's Pub*
THROUGH THE DRINKING GLASS: *Tales From Bulfinche's Pub*
SHADOW OF THE WOLF: *A Tale From Bulfinche's Pub*
REDEMPTION ROAD
BARTENDER OF THE GODS: *Tales From Bulfinche's Pub*

***THE MURPHY'S LORE AFTER HOURS*™ UNIVERSE**
NIGHTCAPS **-** *AFTER HOURS Vol. 1*
EMPTY GRAVES **-** *AFTER HOURS Vol. 2*
THE MUG LIFE **-** *AFTER HOURS Vol. 3*
FAIRY WITH A GUN: *The Collected Terrorbelle*™
FAIRY RIDES THE LIGHTNING: *a Terrorbelle*™ *novel*
TERRORBELLE THE UNCONQUERED
EAD TO RITES: *The DMA Casefiles of Agent Karver*™
RITES OF PASSAGE *(with John French)*
LORE & DYSORDER: *The Hell's Detective*™ *Mysteries*
BY DARKNESS CURSED: *a Hexcraft collection*
BY INVOCATION ONLY: *a Hexcraft novel*

***MURPHY'S LORE STARTENDERS*™**
STARTENDERS - CONSTELLATION PRIZE

MYSTIC INVESTIGATORS SERIES
MYSTIC INVESTIGATORS - MEAN STREETS - FEAR TO TREAD *(COMING SOON)*
OMNIBUS EDITIONS
SHADOWS & BRIMSTON *(includes BULLETS & BRIMSTONE and FROM THE SHADOWS)*
with John French
ONCE UPON IN CRIME *(includes ONCE MORE UPON A TIME and PARTNERS IN CRIME)*
with Diane Raetz

The Playworlds
AS THE GEARS TURN: *Tales From Steamworld*

Xiles
EXILE & ENTRANCE

OTHER BOOKS
NEW BLOOD edited by Diane Raetz & Patrick Thomas
CAMELOT 13 edited by John L. French & Patrick Thomas

THE JACK GARDNER MYSTERIES
THE ASSASSINS' BALL

For Bev and Sally-
who know you had so many problems

Dear Cthulhu,

I work with a woman who is constantly selling things in the office. She claims it's for her kids' band or scouts, but I have my doubts. I don't mind the occasional box of cookies or candy bar, but this woman is selling raffle tickets, clothes, shoes, make-up, toys, and stock investments. She's the supervisor, which makes it difficult to say no. One guy didn't buy anything two weeks in a row and he was fired. She claimed it was because of downsizing, but we posted record revenues that quarter and hired a dozen people. Most weeks I end up buying so much from her that it's Monday afternoon before I'm making any money for myself.

In this job market, I can't afford to lose my job, but I can barely afford to keep supporting her kids either. What can I do?

-Worker ATM Bee

Dear Bee,

Your supervisor is dominant to you, which gives her the right, nay the duty to exploit you to her betterment. I recommend trying to work harder to climb the corporate ladder or get transferred.

Or you could try to counter her by selling things at work to offset your losses. If she tells you to stop, by law the policy would have to exclude all office soliciting equally. Use a video camera to document what happens if she fires you, you will have a nice discrimination lawsuit. If she lets you sell, may I interest you in my *DEAR CTHULHU*™ line of fine products, including action figures, t-shirts, books, fragrances (for him, her, and it), and frozen dinners. Available at wholesale prices if purchased in bulk.

Dear Cthulhu,

I'm a nine-year-old girl and I have a problem with my brother, "Bert". He is terrorizing my dog, who is frightened by thunder to the point where he pees himself. "Puddles" was fine the rest of the time until Bert saw his Niagara Falls imitation during a bad storm. Now Bert saves his paper lunch bag and blows into it, then sneaks up behind Puddles and pops the bag. Poor Puddles is getting in trouble with my parents for wetting the rugs in the house. I told them what Bert was doing, but since they didn't see it and he's denying it, they are reserving judgment. My brother is 11 and bigger than me.

What can I do?

-Little Girl in Georgia With a Real Pisser of a Dog

Dear Little,

Cthulhu would suggest using a rubber band to stop any leakage, but he has gotten in enough trouble with the ASPCA and PETA for the rituals his followers have been using animals for. Do not even get me started on the FBI's harassment of our religious freedom to choose to use human sacrifices in our services.

Your brother appears mean-spirited, spiteful and mean. Despite these good qualities, you seem to have a problem and have asked for Cthulhu's aid. Give him a taste of his own medicine. Get a hold of firecrackers with a long fuse. (If they are illegal in your state, Cthulhu has found almost everything is available on the internet.) After putting Puddles as far away as you can get him, wait until your brother falls asleep. Then sneak into his room and put the firecrackers under his bed and light the fuse. Make sure to run. (Cthulhu is bound to point out that Child Protective Services in your state and your parents would frown and discourage this action. I advise not telling them.)

If this does not work, take martial arts lesson. Kickboxing seems well geared to the female of your species. Then if Bert tries to harass puddles again, you can beat the piss out of him and see if he thinks it is funny then.

Dear Cthulhu,

My husband "Gary" is an addict, but not one with a 12-step program. He's addicted to "U-Bay". It started out simply enough. He sold some toys and things he found in the attic. He was thrilled with the money he made, so he started looking around the house for more things to sell. Suddenly, I was thrilled. Gary started getting rid of things I hated having around—a painting of dogs playing poker, a velvet Elvis, his collection of WC Fields commemorative plates, comics, and a really ugly moose head. He even sold an old car that had been on blocks in the yard since the first year we were married. Gary always said that he was going to fix it up and would never get rid of it, that is until his new addiction kicked in.

Then he started selling other things that I wasn't happy about—a set of china that had been my great grandmother's, my good pearls, my insulin (I'm diabetic), and our TV. It got worse. Our photo albums of our wedding and our children. I hit the roof when I found out he sold his wedding ring, then hit him after I found out he took my engagement ring off of my finger while I was sleeping and sold it to some woman in Topeka.

Our dog and cat both disappeared the same week. Gary claimed they ran away, but I don't believe it. Now I'm very worried because I caught him taking digital pictures of our kids and me.

Please help me.

-On The Auction Block

Dear Block,

You have many options. You could install a program that puts child locks on the computer that won't let him access his accounts. You could buy something from one of his auctions in secret, and then complain to the online auction company that you never got it or it was not what promised. Do this a few times and they might boot him off the service.

You could perform an intervention or you could put his proclivities to good use. Get him a job as a salesman—used cars, makeup, pyramid schemes, campaign fundraising, Amway. Just keep your valuables under lock and key.

Oh, and should he ever put the children up for auction, let me know immediately. I am always looking for a good bargain.

Dear Cthulhu,

I'm a divorce attorney in a small town. Lately, business has dropped off and I'm not sure why. Unfortunately, I am used to making a good income and this is hurting the lifestyle I've become accustomed to. I usually lease a Lexus, but this year I had to get a Volvo.

My buddy just became manager at a local no-tell motel and has mentioned to me exactly who has been renting his rooms and many of them are our town's most prominent citizens. No, I can't prove this as they all pay cash and sign in as John Smith, but there is a way. The cheating husbands and wives all have regular schedules and if would be easy for me to stake out the place and take photos with my digital camera. Then I could burn a CD and send it to the cuckolded spouse anonymously so as not to anger the movers and shakers in my town. I would also time it with a postcard mailing advertising my services.

I know this skirts on the borderlines of ethical and legal conduct, but I need the business. Do you think it would work?
-Scheming Shyster In San Bernardino

Dear Shyster,

Shakespeare said first we must kill all the lawyers, but Cthulhu disagrees. I need someone out there to make me look good by comparison.

Humans are a jealous, vindictive lot, but the bunch of you had to have at least some good qualities. Your plan may work on some, but not all. Often spouses are aware of their worse half's indiscretions and choose to ignore it out of fear of change, embarrassment, or losing a cushy deal where someone else is paying the bills. With these, you may need to go a step further. Sent copies of the photos to the local paper, or even better, the local gossip. Distribute pictures to their families and friends. A good way would be to hide them in the bulletins at their church or house of worship. (If they worship Cthulhu, for a small fee I'll let you put it in our bulletin. And I will have a discussion with the cheater. Cthulhu takes vow breaking very seriously. If they will break a vow to their spouse, what is to keep them from breaking their vows to Cthulhu? Besides pain and torture followed by a horrible death and an eternity of pain.)

Dear Cthulhu,

I am a heterosexual man with a secret. At least two times a week I sneak out to a local gay bar. I do this not because of any closeted tendencies, but because they have the most amazing food. Because of the great grub, they started having a rush of straight customers, which took tables away from their intended clientele. They started charging a $15 cover to get in for lunch for non-gays. For dinner, it's $25. It has cut down on the riff-raff. The problem is I love their food too much to stop going and I can't afford the cover and the meal, so I started behaving in an effeminate manner. It's been enough to get me in. The few times I bump into my restaurant buddies outside, they figure I'm just in the closet and they don't say anything so they don't accidentally out me.

The problem is the local paper did an article on the place while I was there and took pictures of me. I'm worried my wife and kids will see them and get the wrong idea.

What can I do to keep my lunches and my family?
-Metrosexual In Minneapolis

Dear Metro,

Easy. See if they deliver. If not, decide which is more important. If it is your family, then stop going. If it is the food, leave them and change your lifestyle. I just got a letter from another of my readers from your area who was complaining he never gets to meet nice men. I could fix the two of you up, assuming you don't mind the fact that he is into sadism and just got out of jail for accidentally leaving his last lover tied up in a basement for two months. He does, however, say he's a good cook, which should be a plus for you.

Dear Cthulhu,

I have a problem when I shower in the morning. My husband leaves for work before me and every day without fail I get into the shower and find hair on my soap. It's not just any soap. It's almond scented and costs $15 a bar.

I know you will probably say just clean it off myself and I do, but the hair is all clingy and it takes a while. It wastes my time and makes me have to get up earlier every day than I should have to. I've talked to my husband, but he won't change. I have a friend who does electrolysis and I'm tempted to drug him and have her do his entire body, but I'm worried that might give him grounds for divorce and I make more than him and may have to pay him alimony.

Any suggestions?

-Hating My Fuzzy Suds in Freemont

Dear Suds,

You actually pay $15 for a bar of soap? Please e-mail me regarding my catalog of human beauty products, some of them actually legal.

The solution is simple. Get your husband his own bar of soap. (My catalog has several for only $10 each, with the scents of blood, liver, gallbladder, and lavender.) Make sure his is a distinctly different color so he will not confuse the two and your marriage will be saved. As if that is a good thing.

Dear Cthulhu,

I recently saw the letter in your column from Scheming Shyster In San Bernardino, the divorce lawyer whose business had fallen off. I too am a divorce lawyer in a small town with the same problem. However, unlike Shyster, I know exactly what happened to my normally steady flow of customers—her name is "Faith". Faith recently hung out a shingle as a marriage counselor and is apparently exceptionally good at her job. Since she opened her practice, divorces have dropped by a whopping 84%.

I tried to talk with her and explain to her that she was hurting my livelihood, taking bread out of my children's mouths, not to mention prime rib, lobster, and caviar. Faith couldn't have cared less. She actually suggested I change specialties to real estate law. I couldn't believe it.

Sadly, unlike Shyster, my town doesn't have a motel that charges by the hour for secret liaisons, so what worked for him won't for me.

Unfortunately, I don't feel it's a good idea for me to kill Faith or even to have it hired out because I'd be one of the police department's first suspects.

What do you think of hiring someone to become her client, then having him drug her water or coffee or whatever and take advantage of her and have pictures taken to make it look like she's the one taking advantage of him? Then distribute them around the town to make her business drop off?

-Bedeviled Barrister In Bayonne

Dear Bedeviled,

Cthulhu is not one for drugging others. You should be able to accomplish what you need through brute force or by instilling fear or not bother. However, Cthulhu realizes that humans do not have my advantages, so you have to do what you must.

Cthulhu suggests two modifications to your plan. Forget the photographs and go straight to video. It would be more effective. Just make sure your camera operator is careful to make it look like she is an active participant. And make sure it takes place in her office and send a copy to your state licensing board. Copulation with a patient is usually enough to have a counselor's license revoked, which will solve your problem quicker.

Dear Cthulhu,

I've been dating a woman "Mambee" for 3 months now, one of a pair of identical twins. Of course, I suggested the typical male fantasy with her sister "Bambee", but Mambee made it clear she wasn't into it, so I gave up on the idea in favor of enjoying the twin I had.

Last week, we went off to Vegas. I got real drunk and woke up the next morning with a hangover and a wedding ring on my finger. When I went to kiss Mambee good morning and ask what happened, I got slapped. It turns out I had somehow married Bambee and she wasn't happy about it and neither was Mambee.

What they say about what happens in Vegas stays in Vegas wasn't true in my case. It followed me home and filed for divorce, trying to get half of everything I own.

Thinking about it afterwards, I realize they had set me up. Otherwise, how had Bambee gotten there? The problem is I'm at a loss for what to do. Any suggestions?

-Double The Trouble But Only Half The Fun

Dear Half,

You are in a predicament. My advice is to try for an annulment based on fraud. If that doesn't work, try for some fraud of your own. First off, hide all your liquid assets in overseas accounts. Next, have a female friend that you trust storm into town and tell them she's your wife than you ran out on and that she is divorcing you and taking you for everything you have and going to use the twins as the grounds for divorce. Have her promise to sue them for mental anguish. For a large fee, Cthulhu will provide a post-dated marriage certificate from my cult to prove your case. The worst that will happen is you will be charged with bigamy, which they hardly ever do for first-time offenders. If you bring up to the DA what really happened, he will probably not even press any charges just to avoid the headache.

May I suggest you get a prenup from this pretend wife ahead of time just to avoid further complications.

If that does not work, try contacting Bedeviled, but hold out for a lower rate. He will cave because he needs the business.

Dear Cthulhu,

My cat gets stuck in our tree at least a couple of times a week. Usually, I call the fire department, but lately, they've expressed their annoyance at having to do it so often. The other night she climbed up my neighbors' tree. It was late and rather than call the fire department, I decided I'd go up after her myself. I will admit the fact that that tree branch was right outside the window of my hot neighbor "Pam" helped motivate me. I mean if I just happened to be up there while she was naked and getting ready for bed, it wouldn't be my fault, now would it?

I saw more than I bargained for. Pam was naked and on top of her husband. I admitted I watched for a while. Pam waited until he was finished and when he started to nod off to sleep, she wrapped a phone cord around his neck and strangled him. They were having a deck put in and the cement was still setting. Pam, still naked, dragged her hubby outside and dumped his body in the wet cement, then got out a trowel and neatened it up. Again, I watched, but c'mon—she was still naked and the full moon lit things up very nicely.

I considered calling the cops but didn't. I had asked Pam out a bunch of times, but she always used the fact that she was married as an excuse to turn me down. I think maybe now I might get another answer, especially if I mention what I saw. The cops are still investigating and I don't think she's been entirely ruled out as a suspect.

The thing is, should I mention what I saw up front or ask without saying anything? It'd be better if she actually liked me for me, but she's so hot in the long run would it really matter?

-Tree Climbing Would Be Widow Humper

Dear Humper,

It would be safer for you to see if she would date you because of who you are, but whatever gets you through the night. I do recommend never falling asleep with Pam or turning your back on her, especially if she or any of your neighbors are having home improvements done.

Dear Cthulhu,

I'm a *HUGE* fan with a very unusual problem. I'm a young male who knows I was born in the wrong body. Despite being a mortal male, I know I was meant to be an Ancient One and due to a cruel trick of fate, I was instead born into a human body.

I've spent the better part of my adult life trying to set right this great wrong. I've tried to have plastic surgeons alter my appearance to what it should be, but none of them will touch me. It's not fair. They'd give me boobs if I wanted, but when I ask for tentacles they have me committed. I was abused by my mother and sisters as a child and have several gender issues, so becoming a woman would be an even greater torture to endure than my current predicament.

I tried to do it myself. I attached bat wings to my back and sewed an octopus to my face. Unfortunately, I couldn't reach to my shoulder blades with needle and thread, so I had to back up against a stapler.

In the end, it didn't work. The staple wounds got infected, although I loved the green color they turned. Also, the octopus flesh rotted and I ended up passing out from the stench. EMT's brought me to the ER and the damned doctors removed my tentacles and wings. They even thought a psycho had done that to me. When I told them I had done it to myself, I was committed again. This place is nothing like Arkham and they won't let me out.

I was hoping you would recognize the greatness of your kind within me and come to my aid. Perhaps you could raze this place to the ground killing all within, except me of course. Then you could help me realize my true potential by hastening my transformation. Failing that, perhaps you could write a letter of recommendation to the board here telling them that I'm not a danger to myself or humanity as a whole. (Wink,

wink.)
Thanks.
-Your Brother in Chaos

Dear "Brother",

Although your ambitions are laudable, they are also laughable. The idea that a lowly human could ascend to become an ancient one is preposterous.

Your plight has however moved me to intervene on your behalf. I have contacted the facility that currently holds you and pulled a few strings, threatened to devour a few souls and they agreed to bypass normal procedures and medical ethics. You are scheduled with a plastic surgeon next week. Sadly, they lack the skill and techniques to successfully do what you want, so I instructed them to do something they were more adept at. You'll be a C cup by Tuesday.

By your next letter, you'll be able to sign as my Sister in Chaos.

Dear Cthulhu,

I recently found out I was adopted when my "mother" needed a kidney transplant. I volunteered to donate one of mine, but when the doctor did a test for compatibility, I flunked and she had to come clean and tell me the whole truth.

I'm devastated. It feels like my whole life is a lie. I want to find my real parents, to find out why they gave me up. Unfortunately, the adoption agency's records are sealed and I don't have enough money to hire a lawyer to get them opened.

Can you help me?

-Living a Lie in Lexington

Dear Lexington,

What a joy it is to hear from you after all these years. I'm happy to tell you I can indeed help you by telling you who your father is—it is I, Cthulhu.

Let me confess the truth, you were conceived during a drunken weekend in Las Vegas. Not that I was drinking, you understand, but those Shriners I devoured were another story...

When you were born, you took after your showgirl mother and sadly looked nothing like me. Your mother was too career-oriented to want to raise a child and in my circles, your appearance would have been a liability and embarrassment, so we felt it was best to give you up for adoption and a chance at a better life. I am sorry it did not work out the way I hoped.

Sadly, your mother is no longer with us. During another drunken Vegas weekend, I accidentally ate her. It was an honest mistake. She was working on her new act and those swinging tassels sure looked like a couple of Shriners, as least with my booze goggles on.

I would love to see you again, although I'm embarrassed

to admit that like your adopted mother, I too am in need of a kidney. And a liver, heart, and spleen. Also, some cocktail sauce. I would be honored for you, my son, to be able to give them to me, your loving father.

You are welcome to come visit me and donate the organs in person. If this is inconvenient for you, I can send some of my followers by to pick them up.

Remember a father's hunger... I mean love knows no bounds.

Dear Cthulhu,

My grandmother recently became a widow and my grandfather didn't exactly provide for her. She was at a family barbecue and telling us she might have to move into a nursing home and she didn't want to. I jokingly told her she should rob a bank. Everyone laughed, but later Grandma pulled me aside and told me I was her favorite granddaughter. She liked my idea and asked me if I'd like to help her knock over a bank. I figured she would back out long before anything happened so I said sure.

Grandma was transformed by the challenge, staking out banks in neighboring cities, learning when they moved their money, researching things on the Internet. I hadn't ever seen her so alive.

The day came. She decided on a bank. Her plan was to hit it about two hours before the armored car came to transfer money to a larger bank. She decided to use her age to her advantage and stole a motorized wheelchair from one of her friends, and an oxygen tank and mask from another. Grandma topped it off with a wig. She got me a padded nurse's outfit, my own wig, sunglasses, and shoes with lifts to make me look taller. She even put cotton balls in our cheeks to make us look heavier.

The bank didn't know what hit them. First, we cut the phone lines so they couldn't sound the alarm. Grandma even found out that the alarm system sent out an alarm if it didn't get a signal every twelve minutes, so she knew how long we had. Grandma motored in, pulled a 12-guage from under the blanket on her lap. I had a pistol. Everyone listened and gave us their cell phones. We got the cash from the vault where it was already packed and waiting, avoiding any paint packs. We had a foldable dolly cart on the back of the wheelchair so we were able to get it all out in one trip. We put everyone in the vault and shut it, figuring it would keep them from following and block any cell phone signals that we missed. We even grabbed out the surveillance video on the way out as we had covered over the ATM cameras with black spray paint on the way in. We loaded the loot into a stolen van—Grandma learned how to hotwire it on V-Tube. She drove up the ramp, pulling the dolly up behind her. I put a closed for Arbor Day sign on the door. Grandma figured nobody really knows what holidays banks closed for and nobody really knows when Arbor Day is, so it would prevent people from getting suspicious about the bank behind closed. I jammed the doors for good measure and drove us away.

We went a few miles to the back of a house on a quiet road that she knew the people were on vacation. We loaded the cash into the trucks of our cars into duffle bags. I dumped the van two towns away, having changed my nurse's outfit for a running suit, but otherwise keeping the rest of the disguise. Grandma picked me up, we went back for my car, returned the wheelchair and oxygen tanks with no one being the wiser.

When we got to her house, we counted up the cash. We got away with over three hundred grand. Grandma would not have to go to a nursing home and I could pay off my student loans and put a down payment on a condo.

We had gotten away clean or so we thought. It turns out one of the customers on the floor had managed to snap a picture with his cell phone. We hadn't taken them because of the GPS some have and didn't want to waste time destroying them. The picture didn't get more than my legs, but it got the oxygen tank and wheelchair. The FBI lab was able to get their serial numbers and track down the friends Grandma had borrowed them from and they've been arrested.

I feel we should confess rather than let two innocent people got to jail. Grandma says we'd be better off pulling another robbery with the same methods so the cops know it wasn't them. I just think she's becoming an adrenaline junkie. What's the right thing to do?

-Bank Robbing Granddaughter In Delaware

Dear Bank,

It is odd, but I so rarely get a question asking about what the right thing to do it. The best, certainly. The right? Not so much. Cthulhu is not sure how to answer. Turning yourselves in appears to be a stupid choice. It serves no real purpose other than to soothe your guilt. The two friends did not keep a good enough watch over their things, so they are partially to blame. And although Cthulhu is not an attorney, I doubt they will be able to charge them without witnesses who can identify them or at least recovering some of the cash

The second robbery idea has much more merit.

Although Cthulhu notes some hypocrisy in your question. You stole and threatened others with deadly weapons. As I understand "right", neither of these things applies. Why the sudden concern now? It seems self-destructive. The best idea for the two of you would be to plant a small number of bills at each of these women's homes for the cops to find. This would end in their being convicted, but the two of you would not have to live with worry until the seven-year statute of limitations ends. Or if you truly feel guilt, wait until the seven years, then confess. The bank may sue you, but at least you would not have to go to prison.

Dear Cthulhu,

I'm in a real pickle of a problem. Recently I went out drinking with my cousins, to the point where I blacked out. I woke up in my aunt's barn, naked except for a torn condom. I was cuddled up with a sheep. I live in a very religious community where this would be frowned upon. I would probably be ostracized and even made fun of.

My cousins think it's hilarious. They call me a dumb hick and even told me that the sheep was in heat and is now in a family way. I mean a human can't impregnate a sheep, right? I kind of think nothing happened and they set up the whole thing, but how can I be sure? I'm too embarrassed to ask my folks. Can you help me?

     -Asking Ewe for Help

Dear Ewe,

I have sad news for you, being as naive... or rather as concerned as you are. Humans can indeed cross breed with sheep. The spawn look like satyrs. Your cousins did nothing. You should have kept it in your pants. Now you have to deal with the consequences. Since you claim a religious upbringing, you have only one choice. Do the right thing and marry the sheep. Do you know how much hay and oats a sheep and litter of satyrs eat every day? And that doesn't come cheap, so you better drop out of school to get a job to support your new family.

Dear Cthulhu,

My brother and I need you to help settle a bet for us. We've always been competitive, add to that we were raised in an abusive home and you can see how we got here.

We have a bet over which of us is the more accomplished serial killer.

A while back, the stress of life was getting to me. I hated my job, my girlfriend was cheating on me, and my car was in the shop more than it was out. Sex and drugs weren't taking away the edge anymore, so I started killing people. At first, it was just to see if I could get away with it. I did. Then it was the guys my girl was sleeping with, then her. I have sixteen confirmed kills to my credit. (Actually, I think I have seventeen, but one was on a camping trip and the woman jumped over a cliff to get away from me. Her body was never found. I think it should count anyway, my brother says no.)

My brother has always been lazy. When he found out what I was doing, he decided to get in on the act and try to out do me. He couldn't be bothered going out and killing his victims one at a time. Instead, he attacked a small frat party. I mean poisoning the keg is kind of wimping out. Twenty-one people died, which he thinks makes him better than me. Really, twenty-two but one was a guy who was rushing his girlfriend to the emergency room and died in a car crash. Since it wasn't a direct result of the poison, I don't think it should count, especially since he won't count my falling woman.

I say he's not even a serial killer. He's a poisoner. What do you say?

    -Real Serial Killer In Santa Barbara

Dear Real,

Cthulhu feels like he is always repeating this, but people should not kill people. That task is reserved for Cthulhu himself or his designated agents.

That being said, as your designated referee, I would count each of your disputed kills. The man in the car died as a result of the chaos your brother caused, so he is responsible. And if your victim does not return to her home and family, I believe it is safe to assume she died in the fall.

As for the bet itself, I agree with you. Your brother is not a serial killer. He is a mass murderer. The difference being his victims were all killed in the same time frame, not interspersed like yours. So, you win the bet.

Unless of course, your brother does it a couple of more times, in which case he would qualify as both a serial killer and a mass murder and his body count would far exceed yours and he would win.

Dear Cthulhu,

I'm not a good person, but it isn't my fault. I'm an addict and my sickness makes me do things I shouldn't in order to get money to support my habit.

I'm addicted to expensive women's footwear. The problem is I'm a man with size 13E feet, so it's difficult and expensive to get anything attractive in my size.

Recently I got a bonus at work, which I was planning to spend on some pumps and leather thigh high boots. Then my wife, "Stacy", gets it in her head that the money should be spent on our kid's braces. I was furious. She could do without braces, even if the other kids had nicknamed her Beaver.

The final straw was when my favorite online big and wide store had a huge sale. I had to get some money. I started looking around the house for things to sell when I noticed a picture of my wife. My wife has very long hair and takes pride in the fact that she hasn't cut it, other than trimming split ends, since she was a teenager. It's thick, wavy, and goes all the way down to her knees. A guy, "Harry", I know makes wigs and has offered my wife three grand for her hair, but she always turned him down.

That night I had my sister-in-law babysit and took my wife out on a bender. Actually, she's a recovering alcoholic and didn't realize until the third drink that there was vodka in her ginger ale. I was having the bartender slip it in. Pretty soon Stacy was blitzed and she passed out on our front lawn. I took some garden shears and cut her locks off. I took them by Harry and had the money put in my MoneyFriend online account. The shoes were on their way to me before Stacy woke up.

She was very upset with her crew cut and the fact that she had been drinking. She didn't remember the previous night, so I told her she had done the drinking on her own and someone must have cut her hair while she was passed out.

Stacy's gotten a little out of control since. The house has gone to pot and she got fired from her job, so I'm short on money again and Big and Wide is having another sale next week.

I've heard the blood bank is playing for donations, but I have a couple of questions. Will they take blood from drunks? Will they be able to figure out I've brought my wife to another place if I have them use separate arms? Will they let me take the blood myself and will they give me a kit for that? I'm thinking of having my daughter donate to the cause since she's wearing a couple of dozen pairs of my shoes on her teeth. She's twelve, so she may be too young to donate, so if I can get it myself, I'll just say it's mine. Do you think it's child abuse?

-Bleeding Family Dry In Bellmore

Dear Bleeding,

It is Cthulhu's understanding that blood must be donated straight from the source. It is probably a safeguard to keep humans like you from killing someone and selling off their blood for fun and profit.

Cthulhu has another option. I would be willing to buy your wife and daughter from you and in exchange, I will give you a gift certificate to your shoe shop for one hundred pairs of shoes. Not only will you be rid of them, but you can turn your daughter's room into a showcase for your footwear. Let me know.

Dear Cthulhu,

My grandfather's been having some health issues and the family decided that he should be put in a nursing home. A couple months ago Gramps asked me if I'd move in with him to help him out.

I'd been living with this woman rent free for about a year but there was a problem. I was supposed to be paying half the rent. She was letting me slide because she thought we were engaged. I mean, I gave her a ring but I was drunk at the time and have no recollection of what I said. I figured if I can't remember proposing, it doesn't count, right? Besides, we never actually discussed it. Well, she did. I just didn't correct her misunderstanding. It's her own fault for not picking up on my signals—I never set a date, picked a best man or any of the usual stuff. I did go to several caterers, but never picked one. I just went because they gave us free grub and it was pretty good stuff so it made for a cheap date. Even the ring should have tipped her off. I won it in one of those crane games with the stuffed animals. It's glass. She didn't even get suspicious when she insisted I have it appraised and we went to the Slushie King next to the jewelry store at the mall and had my buddy Zeke do the appraisal. He told her he usually worked at the jewelry store, but the guy also owned the Slushie King and just had him filling in that day. The appraisal said it was worth ten grand—I don't even have a job. Where'd she think I came up with that kind of scratch? Besides the appraisal was done on the back of a Slushie King receipt. I can't be held at fault because she's dumb. Yet she's blaming me and tried to kill me with a steak knife when she caught me having sex with her sister.

In short, I needed a place to live in a hurry when Gramps asked, so I agreed. I wasn't thrilled about it because I have to cook, do the laundry, and take him to his doctor appointments and stuff, but he is family. The problem is gramps got lucky with this slutty senior chick and he invited her to move in with us. I was happy the old guy was getting some and I didn't have to watch Matlock re-runs all the time. Plus, Slutty did the laundry and the cooking.

The problem came one night when I got home late from the bar. I was kind of drunk and had the munchies and Slutty must have heard me. Gramps was out cold. She comes into the kitchen in this tiny silk nightie. There were things hanging in ways I'd never seen before and would be happy never seeing again. Worse, I was seeing double so I saw twice as much. Slutty came onto me. Instead of telling her the idea of doing her turned my stomach, I turned her down gently, telling her I couldn't mess with her on account of she was Gramp's whore.

Slutty said she understood and even poured me a beer. After I drank it, the world started spinning. Before I knew what was happening, Slutty had thrown me down, ripped off my pants and was riding me like a wild bronco. What was worse was it was totally amazing. What age and gravity had taken away from Slutty, time and experience had made up in spades. She did things to me that I never knew were possible.

The problem is she's still interested. And I think I am too, at least after I get drunk, but what about Gramps? Slutty is his whore. Is it wrong to keep doing her or should I stop out of respect? Or should I just let her keep slipping me ruffies so I can blame it on that? Not to mention get free drugs and beer? Or if I try it straight, how do I get past the wrinkles and sagging parts?

-Wants Wrinkly Woman In Warsaw

Dear Wants,

It seems that you use drinking as an excuse to justify the things you do. This is a poor excuse. You are responsible for your own actions. If you drink and propose to a woman, unless you speak up when you sober up, you are still engaged. Your girlfriend's stupidity does not enter into it, although it does explain why she said yes. Yes, Slutty drugged and took advantage of you, which you could report to your local police. If you choose to take any beverage from her, you should expect that it will be drugged. If this gets you in the mood and you are fine with that, there is no problem. In fact, I understand. Many of the women my followers bring to Cthulhu need drugs as well before they can relax enough for sex. I am told that I am rather intimidating, both in bed and out, although eventually, they learn to appreciate what all these tentacles can do to and for them, but Cthulhu digresses.

As for your grandfather, it is disrespectful. Human men have been known to fight and kill over their women. As you are younger and he is in a wheelchair, I think you would be the victor in a fight, however, in anger, your grandfather may use a weapon. In my experience, the weakest individual with a gun is more powerful than the strongest person without one. If he finds out, you should move out immediately. I doubt your excuse of being drunk and drugged will help you with an old man scorned.

Also, considering your history, you should avoid the alcohol with Slutty or in the throes of passion, you may end up engaged again. Although if she is heavily insured, this could pay off for you after a few years. It is my experience that sex and money can make some people overlook anything, including wrinkles and sagging parts.

Dear Cthulhu,

My brother and I are the fourth generation in our family to live on Welfare, although technically, we're not the ones the checks are made out to.

We've never known who our fathers were. Our mother ran off with some bum and dumped us on Grandma years ago. She wasn't so bad to live with, except for that old lady smell.

Four months ago, Granny died, but we didn't tell anyone because we knew social services would take us away because we're minors. Granny's checks keep coming, so we forge her name and cash them. We usually ran to the check cash place anyway, so she didn't have to miss her soaps.

Our problem is the corpse stink is way worse than the old lady smell ever was. The neighbors are starting to ask questions. The project is too busy for us to get her body out of the building without risking being noticed by a neighbor. We have several questions. Do you have any suggestions on how to sneak the body out? What can we do about the smell? Because other than that, we have a sweet deal. We even stopped going to school and we don't want to mess things up.

-Rooming with a Dead Granny

Dear Rooming,

Devouring the corpse always works for me, but most of you humans seem to have a problem with cannibalism. Worse, you might somehow consider eating your Granny an incestuous meal.

Try sealing her inside some industrial strength garbage bags and putting that inside one of those large sealing containers people store their clothes in. Then spend some of your ill-gotten gains on incense and air freshener. Or research mummification at your local library. Don't do it on the internet from your home computer, because that information can be subpoenaed and used against you if it ever comes to a trial. They may let you slide for keeping a dead body, but the government will come after you for taking their money.

Dear Cthulhu,

With all due modesty, I am probably the greatest unknown serial killer of modern times and therein lies my problem. My body count is fast approaching four figures, but I'm getting older–I'll be 64 next summer. In any other profession, I'd be nearing retirement age and to be honest, I'm considering throwing the towel in. I've been doing this since I was 10. I'm getting old and have a bad back, so disposing of bodies isn't as easy as it used to be.

Without a doubt, I'm far better than Manson, Dahmer, Gasey and the rest. For one thing, I never got caught, but they have all the spotlight, fame and glory. I want best sellers to be written about me, TV movies chronicling my exploits. I want my face on a serial killer trading card.

Unfortunately for that to happen, I'd have to confess, which means jail or worse. I don't want to do time or dance with a needle, so tell me how to get credit without being caught.

    -Killer Sick of the Shadows

Dear Killer,

Before I address your question, Cthulhu would again like to state his opinions on human on human killing. I am against it. Humans should not kill each other for fun, profit or food. That right belongs to Cthulhu alone. If we ever met, I will have to slay you on principle alone. Not that Cthulhu needs an excuse to kill.

That being said, use your head. Send letters to the papers and news services, using appropriate precautions, telling of your dark deeds. Include proof. Give yourself a catchy name—strangler and slasher are perennial favorites. You will gain the notoriety you crave. However, unless you are foolhardy enough to include a personal photo, your dream of being on a trading card with still elude you.

If you would like to send Cthulhu your address, I would be happy to take you out in a dark alley and forever end your crimes against the proper order of the universe.

Dear Cthulhu,

I'm in my eighties and have bad lungs and a bad heart. The doctors tell me I don't have long. I'm not rich, but I've made some good investments and am very comfortable. Ever since they found out I'm not long for this world my son and daughter have been spending more time visiting, like I can't figure out why. The whelps want my money. I've never really liked either. Only had the brats because my wife wanted kids and I wanted peace. I was a good husband until she died five years ago. Since the doctors gave me the news, I decided to treat myself, so I've been dating Candi, a twenty-one-year-old stripper and how sweet it is. I have no illusions about her having feelings for me. Like my kids, she's in it for my money. I buy her nice things—she likes shiny objects—and for what I'm getting, it's the best value

I've made up two phony wills to get what I want from all involved, but not sure what to actually do with my estate. I'm thinking about leaving it to charity just to tick them all off. What do you think?

-Going Out In Style In Sacramento

Dear Going,

I think leaving your estate to charity is a wonderful idea. It can help so many and setting it up before your passing for annuities can give many tax benefits. If I may suggest my cult's Dear Cthulhu Fund for Widows and Orphans. It is a fully registered religious non-profit and helps take the worry away from my human sacrifices at the end. After all, in their last moments, they have enough on their minds and it makes me happy to do anything I can do to ease their passing.

Dear Cthulhu,

I've killed three men and I'm afraid I may kill again. It's not my fault, not exactly. I live in a nursing home. Recently my doctor put me on hormone therapy for my hot flashes and it's made me hornier than a teenager. Viagra is readily available here so I've been taking advantage of the situation, rather vigorously I'm afraid. We had some good times before the end, although I dislocated Stan's total hip. He didn't complain though He didn't complain though cause I managed to put it back in the next morning before the doctor on call could. I can honestly say all three men died with a smile. I've never liked to cuddle afterwards, which is fortunate. I've managed to sneak out of their rooms and get back to my own without getting caught by the staff.

I've got a date with Barry this weekend and I'm worried. He's the last attractive man left. The new residents they brought in to fill in the empty beds have all been women. I'm not that horny.

I'm not willing to cancel my date, but I don't want Barry to croak. Any suggestions?

-Hot To Trot Granny in Boca

Dear Granny,

You need to take better care of your boy toys. You cannot expect these elderly gentlemen to suddenly behave like they were twenty again. Get them involved in physical activities at your home like senior aerobics. Take them on long walks—it is not just romantic, it is a practical cardiovascular activity. Also start out slowly the first few times, build up their endurance. That or try to work on some of the staff, but it is my understanding the older of your gender are less attractive, so monetary gifts or less attractive males may be necessary.

Dear Cthulhu,

My parents are trying to ruin my life. I'm twelve and I love video games. I have Z-box, Funstation 4, and the Wee-wee. In addition to my twenty bucks a week allowance I'm supposed to get a brand-new game every week, but I haven't gotten even one in the last three weeks. My Dad says it's because he and Mom got laid off from their jobs on Wall Street four months ago and we don't have the money. And then he has the nerve to tell me I must have a dozen games I've never even opened. I told him he was wrong. I even checked. I only had eleven.

Now he's stopped my allowance and took away my cell phone because I went a little over on my texting and we ended up with a $300 bill. Worse, he's trying to spend time with me. Apparently, he thinks he thinks he neglected me for years because he chose to focus on his job instead of me. He wants to make things better. I say if it ain't broke, don't fix it. I even threatened to stop doing my chores if I didn't get my games, phone, and cash back. He laughed. Who knew he realized I didn't have any chores. Now he wants to give me some.

Now my dad is trying to give me some BS story about us living paycheck to paycheck and being two months behind on the mortgage. What a load of garbage. Hasn't he heard about the government bailouts? Not my fault if he can't figure a way to get a piece of that action, now is it? He tells me if I want money I should work for it or put some of my stuff up on U-Bay. I'm thinking about running away so I don't have to deal with this crap anymore. What do you think?

-Entitled in Encino

Dear Encino,

Reading your letter reminds Cthulhu why so many creatures, myself included, eat their young. Besides them being both tender and tasty that is.

Families should pull together in times of crisis, yet you have no idea of what that even means. It gives Cthulhu hope that mankind will yet destroy itself. I have a hundred dollars down in a pool that says it will probably start with a fight over a parking space.

At such a tender age, being out on one's own is filled with obstacles and fraught with dangers. Predators will want to use and abuse you for their own twisted and nefarious purposes. You must come up with ways to obtain food, shelter, and clothing. Safety against the elements, disease and wild animals will no longer be a given. There will be a lack of continued education to better yourself so you can contribute something back to society. Obviously, since you have not learned anything of importance in your dozen years of existence, Cthulhu doubts the last one will affect you much. Although this is as much your parent's fault as it is yours. If they bothered to take the time to bring another life into this world, they should at least take the time to make sure it does not turn out like you. Although I suspect you may have been an accident, perhaps one where your mother did not realize she was pregnant until your head started crowning in some restroom stall.

You should start packing your things immediately and head out on your own. Buy a bus ticket as far away from home as you can afford. Do not worry if you spend all your money on it for a human of your caliber will get what is coming to him in short order. I recommend leaving your parents a note telling them you are leaving. This way they do not waste the police's time searching for you and they will know what has happened. I am certain they will be saddened at first, just as I am sure I will never understand why. Eventually, they will come to grips and realize not only is it for the best but that their lives are a happier place for it. It will likely take at least a week before they realize how quiet and whine-free their home is with you gone. It should take you less time to realize so many other things.

I would say good luck, but Cthulhu does not like such outright and flagrant displays of dishonesty.

Dear Cthulhu,
Why does the universe mock me at every turn?
-At The End Of My Rope

Dear Rope,
Mainly because you are an easy target. Stop with the drama, quit whining and things could get better, but probably not. Oh, your rope is frayed as well.

Dear Cthulhu,

I was recently hurt in an accident and lost my job. Then I found out my girlfriend of two years is a nitrous oxide whore. She gets her ha-has putting out for laughing gas. Apparently, there's a lot of hard up dentists and they want cash as well as her personal services. I'm having trouble paying my bills and things around my apartment, like my TV and U-pod, keep disappearing. My girlfriend says it wasn't her and I believe her. Well, not really, but I'm kind of ugly and she's the only woman who I've been with in the last five years and the sex is better than TV. Well, daytime TV. She usually just lies still, which is sad, but not as bad as when she'd get up to go fix herself a sandwich in the middle and forget to come back.

The problem is she keeps telling me to kill myself. She thinks I have a life insurance policy with her as the beneficiary. I did, but it was through the job that I no longer have. She also wants me to sign a form giving her permission to harvest my organs for sale. I want to know is that even legal? And if it is, is she allowed to do it herself? She claims she is because she went to one day of dental hygienist school, but it seems far-fetched to me. I guess I should have suspected her problem then—she was kicked out for using up all the school's nitrous oxide,

Things came to a head the other night when I woke to find her standing over me with a marker, a steak knife, and a copy of the Operation kids' game. She was holding it like it was an instruction book. She claims she wasn't doing anything but there was an outline over my liver and funny bone in permanent marker matching up to the game.

I've since stopped letting her spend the night because I'm afraid for my safety. If I had any self-respect, I'd dump her. I don't so I'm not, but I don't want to die. Do I tell her the truth

about not having the life insurance policy anymore and risk losing her or keep going on and risk her killing me?
-Jobless and Shameless in Shohola

Dear Jobless,

It never ceases to amaze Cthulhu the depths humans will sink to in order to procreate. First, absolutely tell her about the policy lapsing. This way she loses the motivation to kill you. Since you want to maintain your procreation activities, I suggest you buy a large stock of nitrous oxide and dish it out to her in exchange for services rendered. Yes, it is illegal to have nitrous oxide with the intent to use it without a medical or dental license. However, it can be bought to use as an injection for fuel in cars. Do this and hide it away, because otherwise, I suspect she will wipe out your stock if given a chance, which will, of course, take away her motivation to become amorous toward you.

Dear Cthulhu,

I'm adopted. My parents have always been honest with me about it. I always tried to be a good daughter and I can't imagine better parents. Still, there is a part of me that wants to know where I came from and why they gave me up. Plus, all that family medical history stuff could be important some day.

I approached the adoption agency that placed me with my family and they refused to tell me anything. I knew for a fact that they had helped put other adoptees in touch with their birth mothers, but they wouldn't with me. When pressed all they would tell me is that it was for the best.

I'm not one to take no for an answer, so I got a job working for their cleaning company. It took three weeks for me to locate my file. Yeah, I know it was technically stealing but their office has never looked so clean, so I figured it was a fair trade. Besides, it was *my* file.

It took me another couple of weeks to track down my birth mother and another week to get up the nerve to go knock on her door. I'm not sure what I was expecting, certainly not a hug but when I told the woman who I was, but she flipped out. Called me the Anti-Christ and sprayed me in the face with a fire extinguisher. Then she smacked me in the skull with the metal canister. I ran for my car and got away, but not before she smashed in my windshield.

It turns out she didn't know I was put up for adoption. She thought I was the spawn of the devil and tried to drown me. Several times. Apparently, it was because of a birthmark I have that kind of looks like three "6's". Finally, her minister stepped in and took me away. The reverend got her to sign the adoption papers by lying to her and saying it was a waiver so he could kill me for her, which explained her extreme reaction and why the agency didn't want to help me find her. And why I have a fear of the water.

The problem is now that she knows I'm alive, she has been stalking me to try and finish what she started when I was a baby. I made the mistake of telling her my name and where I lived when I introduced myself so she knows where to find me. After she met me at my door with a meat cleaver, I got a restraining order, but my brake lines have been cut twice. And my car blew up. Luckily, I had a remote starter and it was a chilly morning or I would have been hamburger.

The cops say they can't prove it's her. As for the meat cleaver incident, there were no other witnesses and they didn't find the cleaver, so it's my word against hers. I've also found scorpions in my bed and a rattlesnake in my toilet bowl. Apparently, rattlers can't swim because it was dead when I found it, but I can't take this anymore. My boyfriend went to have a chat with her to make her stop and nobody's heard from him since. The cops think he just took off.

What can I do to stop this psycho woman?

-Afraid of a Bad Mama Jammer in Bayonne

Dear Bayonne,

Well, we can certainly assume she is mistaken about your identity or you would have smitten her by now. This argument could be made to a sane person, of which it does not sound your birth mother qualifies. You could move to another city and assume a new identity, but she might be able to track you unless you break off all contact with your loved ones.

Your best bet is to bring the plight of your missing boyfriend to the attention of your local media, particularly the newspapers and TV news. Explain how he has gone missing. Tell them the tale of how you went looking for your birth mother and found a raging psychopath instead. They will eat it up with headlines like BIRTH MOTHER TRIES TO KILL ANTI-CHRIST

DAUGHTER. You can use the attention to make the police get a search warrant to look for your boyfriend's remains. If they find him, she goes to jail and you don't have to worry for 25 to life. If not, a story like this could very easily go national. Tabloids will start asking her why she slept with the devil. It stands to reason if she believes you are the daughter of the devil and she was your mother that she must have procreated with the devil. She will either try to hide from them or turn her murderous rage on the tabloid reporters where it might do some good. (Cthulhu would like to re-state that he does not approve of humans slaying each other. It is Cthulhu's right alone to cull the human herd. However, if it must be done, it might as well benefit society in some way.) Either way, it distracts her from you. Plus, if there is enough publicity, you may be able to turn it into a reality television show called The Devil's Daughter and make enough to hire private security to keep you safe. Until then, always have someone you do not like start your car.

Dear Cthulhu,

My husband is divorcing me and I think he's being a hypocrite for doing it. He's a minister, but in a sect that allows divorce, so that's not the hypocritical part. He's always going on about how he is doing God's work all the time, but when I do the same thing he wants to call off our marriage.

Our church is against gay marriage, so when "Bruce", one of our parishioners, announced he was going to marry a man my husband immediately counseled him. They had several sessions, but nothing my husband said could change his mind, including telling him he would no longer be able to attend our church. My husband viewed this as a personal failure, thinking that he lost one of the souls the Lord entrusted to him. He was quite depressed over it.

I thought I might succeed where my husband failed. He might have a collar, but I had a push-up bra and a butt that could stop traffic. I figured I could bring Bruce back from the dark side and into the light. With that in mind, I dressed in my sexiest lingerie under a trench coat and went to his apartment. Let me tell you, I worked it. Inside of five minutes I had him riding hard back on the path to righteousness. Then his fiancé "James" walked in. Things were tense there for a few minutes, but I figured I could bring salvation to two just as easily as one and before long James had seen the light at the end of the tunnel. I got biblical on both of them, then under and between them. I saved each of them three times that night and if I needed any extra proof the amount of times they screamed "Oh God!" gave it to me. I went home and slept the sleep of the just.

I was expecting them to call off the wedding. Instead, I found out they were hosting their own webcast about the wedding and had caught my naked evangelizing on a webcam. Half the town saw it and the other half found out about it by the next day. My husband kicked me out of the rectory and filed for divorce, despite my explanation that I was trying to save their souls by giving them a piece. Of heaven that is.

Would you please explain to my husband that what I did was for the greater good and he should just suck it up. I'm certainly willing to.

-Woman Positioning to be a Missionary in Minnesota

Dear Missionary,

You have asked for Cthulhu's advice, so I will dispense on the lecture on your poor choice of religion. You will never catch Cthulhu asking his followers to chow down on a piece of my tentacle. But I digress.

I have a passing familiarity with the tenets of your religion and it is my understanding that it actually actively discourages copulation outside of marriage. As a member of that faith, you are bound to follow their rules, not make up your own. In addition to your unfortunate devotion to your faith, you have made vows to your husband, which you have broken. In my cult, he could publicly flog you and offer you up as a sacrifice to me. In his mind, his only option is the one he is taking, which is to divorce you.

My advice is to quit your religion so you can do what you like without hypocrisy. You may also have much success forming your own religion if copulation is your path to enlightenment.

Dear Cthulhu,

I am a bisexual man who works for a married couple. The husband "Hans" and I went away on a business trip together and the hotel messed up our reservations. By the time we got there, they only had one room with a full-size bed. Rather than making me sleep in the rental car, Hans figured I could sleep on the floor. Then he felt bad for me and told me to get into the bed with him. One thing led to another and Hans and I started seeing each other, going hot and heavy, especially in the office when his wife, "Gretel" wasn't around.

Then Hans went on another trip and didn't take me because he was going to be staying at his sister's house. Gretel and I were in the office when she confessed to me that she thought Hans was cheating on her. Any other day, I would have defended him, but I was upset he didn't take me with him, so I told her she might be right. Gretel broke down and cried on my shoulder. One thing led to another and we did it on her desk. We spent the rest of the weekend doing it anywhere else we could find.

Now I'm seeing both of them. When one of them leaves, the other attacks me. It was fun at first, but now I can't get any of my work done and I'm falling behind. There are times I can't keep, well, "up" with the workload. Worse, I leave exhausted. Some days I get home and can barely have sex with my own wife or my male mistress.

The problem is next week, both Hans and Gretel are going to separate conferences and want me to choose which one I'm going to. I don't want to go with either. Frankly, I could use the rest, but I don't want to hurt either of them, especially since both could fire me.

What should I do?

-Manwhore in Manchester

Dear Manwhore,

Could you get another job easily? If so, you may want to consider it. Other than fatigue, you seem to be enjoying the situation. Allow Cthulhu to make some suggestions. Tell each of your bosses that you are having trouble keeping up with your workload because of your extracurricular activities and see if you can get them to hire you an assistant. That will give you more time. As for the fatigue, may Cthulhu suggest large doses of caffeine and male potency enhancing drugs. That should solve your problems, so long as one thing doesn't lead to another with your new assistant.

Dear Cthulhu,

My boyfriend is into golden showers and wants me to join him, but I'm not so sure. It doesn't seem healthy to me.

What's your take?

-Unsure of Golden Opportunity in Seattle

Dear Unsure,

Cleanliness is a good thing, especially as the stench of you humans is everywhere on this sad little world, so showering is a good thing. However, if the water coming out of your tap is not clear, but golden, you may have some heavy mineral deposits in your ground water. Probably sulfur. I recommend having it tested and installing a filter on your water tank. It may be safe to shower with, but I wouldn't recommend drinking it.

Dear Cthulhu,

I'm a college student and my roommate is a pain in the butt. "Tammy" is little Ms. Perfect. She has a 4.0, is on full scholarship, volunteers almost every day of the week, and is dating the captain of the lacrosse team. Tammy was even growing her hair to donate to Hair for Whores, an organization that was helping out local prostitutes that were attacked by the Nair Avenger, some religious nut who figured he could stop hookers if they were all bald.

I ate her food out of our fridge and wore her favorite outfits. It didn't phase her. I tried to sleep with her boyfriend, but he turned me down flat. Finally, I decided to do something drastic. Tammy eats jello like it's going out of style, so I replaced her snack with some I made with vodka instead of water. She ate an entire bowl, which was equal to about eight shots and passed out. I shaved her bald and sold her hair to a wig maker.

When she woke up, she thought the Nair Avenger had attacked her. She organized the hookers to demand the police do something. She ended up capturing him herself and now she has a book and movie of the week deal worth millions.

Living with her is driving me even more nuts than before. What can I do?

> \- Malicious Roommate in Montana

Dear Malicious,

The solution is so simple it makes Cthulhu wonder how you actually got into college. Daddy built the university a library, did he?

Move out to another dorm and you need never see Tammy again. You can use the money from the wig maker for moving expenses.

Dear Cthulhu,

I've been dating "Ted" for two years and things had been going well. I thought he was the one until the day I saw him and my sister sneaking off together in the middle of the day. They thought I was going to be at work, but I took a long lunch to surprise him with a quickie. Imagine my surprise to see her pull up ahead of me at his house and go right up to the door. He opens it, hugs her and they go inside and close the door. You didn't have to draw me a picture, but you could have knocked me over with a feather. My boyfriend cheating on me with my own sister!

I wasn't going to let either one of them get away with it. First, I went to Ted's brother's apartment. As soon as he opened the door, I pushed him inside and went after him like a nymphomaniac who just spent forty days in the desert. Next, I went to his father's house wearing nothing but a raincoat and a smile. When we were done, his father had a smile too. Then I visited his two best friends at the same time if you get my drift. And last but not least, I went to my sister's husband. He was the only one to tell me no until I told him that his wife was cheating on him. He didn't believe me until I showed him the video footage of them going inside together I took on my cell. I helped him get over his grief and over me.

But just getting even with the two of them wasn't enough. I needed to rub their noses in it. Luckily, I have a huge memory card on my phone and took videos of my encounters and posted it on X-Tube and sent e-mails to not only the cheaters but our friends and family. There were so many hits my video montage was the number one watched of the whole week. I think my splicing was artistically done and setting it to the song that keeps repeating *if you like it, you should have put a ring on it* helped.

Ted and Sis were really PO'ed. I told them they got what

they deserved. Ted was so livid he could only stutter. Sis told me I was an idiot. It turns out they weren't having an affair. Ted had asked Sis to help him pick out an engagement ring to give to me. The hug was just their excitement.

I told them I didn't believe them until Ted pulled out the ring. The rock had to be 2 karats easy, real high quality in all four C's. It was the type of diamond ring I had always dreamt of since I was a little girl, but Sis knew that. I admit I started to tear up. I said yes to his unanswered question, but when I reached out to take the ring he pulled it back and told me to go to hell.

I apologized but neither of them would accept it. I even took the video off the web, but the damage was done. Neither Ted or Sis will speak to me. Worse, my Mom and the rest of the family are siding with them. Sis is even using the clips of me and her husband to file for divorce.

I screwed up, both literally and big time. I realize now that I love Ted and want to spend the rest of my life with him. How do I get him to forgive and forget about this? Can I ever regain his trust? What should I do?

    -Fumbling Fornicator In Fredericksburg

Dear Fumbling,

In Cthulhu's experience, humans with any modicum of self-respect for themselves who truly care for their partner have difficulty getting past infidelity, with the possible exception of some who adhere to an alternate lifestyle belief system involving partner sharing or polygamy. Those who either do not care for themselves or their partner have been known to encourage these activities with their partner, but there is no real love there.

For you to have committed so many infidelities in rapid succession and then to have made them so public without regard for any of the others involved, including your partners and former boyfriend, will make it especially difficult for him to forget. This will be even further compounded by the fact that a quick web search shows that your little film has been archived on no less than eleven other sites, which means evidence of your cheating acts will likely forever be available for viewing on the internet. Can you imagine the conversation Ted might one day have to have with your teenage children to explain the existence of said video? I would imagine he already has considered this scenario, which makes it more unlikely that he would consider reconciliation.

As for what you could do to regain his trust, Cthulhu does not know if there is anything you could do short of lobotomizing him, but a drooling idiot is probably not the type of mate you are looking for. You could also consider learning hypnosis or drugging him, but the odds against him letting you close enough to try either are considerable.

It is probably best for all involved if you simply move on, preferably by changing your name and leaving town. However, your little movie does show some skill so you might want to consider a career in adult filmmaking as either a director or actress.

Dear Cthulhu,

I'm a 22-year-old man and I've slept with a stuffed animal, my Boo-boo Bear since I was a baby. I realize it's a little weird, but it's worked well for me. I always wake rested and I've never had insomnia. It was a great system until "Shanna".

Shanna and I had been dating for a few months and our relationship progressed in the normal way and we started sleeping together. At first, it was at her place, so I made an excuse to get up and leave in the wee hours of the morning, saying I had to get home to get ready for work. Once there, I'd catch a couple of hours with Boo-Boo Bear. This worked great until she decided to start coming over to my place and packing an overnight bag. I tried to cuddle Shanna instead, but it wasn't the same. Don't get me wrong, in most ways it's better, but somewhere deep inside, it wasn't the same. I wasn't sleeping well, which started to affect me at work. I fell asleep on the job but luckily woke up before getting caught or before I crashed the bus I drive. I didn't want to get fired, so I'd wait until Shanna was asleep and get Boo-boo Bear. I slept well for the first time in a week. As soon as the alarm went off, I threw my bear under the bed so Shanna wouldn't see. It worked for a week, then I made a mistake. On Saturday, neither of us had to get up for work so we didn't set an alarm. Shanna woke up before me and saw me sleeping with the bear.

She got me up by yelling. Seems she was upset by it, jealous almost. I explained that my feelings for her and Boo-boo are very different and one does not affect the other. Shanna doesn't care and is demanding I get rid of Boo-Boo. I don't think I can. I'm worried I'll never sleep well again. On the other hand, I'm worried if I break up with Shanna, I'll never have sex again and Boo-boo is not a substitute for that, especially since I don't think of him that way. Plus, he's a guy bear, which would kind of bother me. I really like the sex. I was a virgin before we met and believe it or not, I'm kind of nerdy.

I'm torn between being tired all the time and my job suffering for it, but having sex every night or being well rested but lonely. What should I do?

-Bear Necessities in Baltimore

Dear Bear,

You have developed a rather extreme attachment to a stuffed animal. However, for you, it has been functional. Perhaps a compromise could be reached. The bear could be put on a nearby shelf or you could purchase a headboard with bookshelves and leave the bear there. Another option is on a nightstand, where you could reach out and touch it, but still, keep it out of the bed. Cthulhu would suggest cutting a piece out of it to hold, but with your attachment that might prove too traumatic. If Shanna will not agree to compromise, then you will have to deceive her for your own benefit, like all good relationships. Put the bear on your side of the bed between the mattress and box spring. This way you can sleep and take comfort from being near him and your procreation partner doesn't know. Or put him inside your pillow and sew it back up. Cthulhu doubts you would get in trouble for cuddling a pillow and if you do get questioned, blame it on habit.

One other thing to keep in mind is regular sex typically does not last in a human relationship, so given time you may find more comfort in the bear. Also, in Cthulhu's experience, there are humans who will procreate with anything, so your fear of no longer having sex is probably unfounded, provided you are not horribly disfigured. Even then, you could find partners, although some of them might find Boo-boo Bear even more attractive than you, but at least you would not have to hide him.

Dear Cthulhu,

I have a problem. I recently got my wife to take me back, which is good because I don't like to work and she supports me when we're together. "Daisy" is big into animal rights nonsense and we got a kitten so she had to have it spayed and neutered. She made me do it because I didn't have a job. I used to tell her putting up with all her crap was a full-time job, but that was why she kicked me out the last time so I kept my mouth shut this time and took the cat. Problem was, the vet was next door to an OTB and I had a hot tip on a horse in the fourth race so I put Fluffy's surgery money on the nose to win. Turns out the tip wasn't so hot and I lost. Not wanting wifey to be pissed at me, I taped some gauze to the cat's stomach and took her home, telling my wife it was done. She became suspicious that I brought the cat home that night. Apparently, normally they keep the animal overnight. Who knew? Anyway, Fluffy's an inside cat, so I figured I'd be safe. Wrong. The little hairball got in heat and ran off one day while I was holding the door to talk to these two cute Jehovah's Witnesses I was trying to convince to come in and show me what begot meant. The cat took off and so did the women.

Fluffy stayed out all night, apparently whoring it up because she came back pregnant. Or at least I think she did. I tried one of my wife's home pregnancy tests on the cat, although I have no idea why my wife has them. We haven't had sex in months. I was relieved when it was negative until I found out it didn't work on animals. I broke in and stole one from the vet's office, but collecting the urine was hell. Daisy still hasn't stopped complaining about the smell in the living room or asking me about the scratches on my arms.

I think the test was positive, but I forgot to steal the instructions. I don't want to tell my wife because she threatened to kick me out if Fluffy didn't come back the night she was slutting it up. If she finds out I faked the neutering, I'm out on the street. I can't just get rid of the cat because she'd still kick me out. Ditto on killing it. If the cat is preggers, what are my options?

What's a guy to do?

-Pussycat Problem in Peekskill

Dear Peekskill,

Lie, but come clean at the same time. If you harm the cat or the kittens, your wife will never forgive you and when she kicks you out this time there will be no hope for reconciliation because every time she looks at you, she will see an animal abuser.

Your best bet is to tell her what you did, leaving out the part about betting on the horse. Instead tell her you felt forced neutering was wrong, that when you brought the cat to the vet all you could picture was someone forcing your wife to be neutered and you could not force that on another living being. These are the type of phrases that get to animal rights activists. Tell her you donated the cash to PETA. Now explain that the thought of bringing all those little kittens into the world and not being able to care for them has finally made you realize that she was right. Grovel, apologize, and promise to find homes for all the kittens. And to make it easier on you, there is a restaurant near you that makes the most delicious Kung Pu Kitten. They will give the kittens a good home until it is time to serve them up.

Dear Cthulhu,

My roommate "Art" is an artist. So am I, but he's got more talent and imagination than I do. Sadly, both of us have struggled in obscurity for years, but lately, that's changed. Unfortunately, that's because Art died in a bizarre paint explosion. When they took his body away, it left its own outline. The explosion was caught on video and was shown on all the local news networks and has had millions of hits on MeTube.

I started putting a few of his piece up on U-bay and there were bidding wars. I made a mint. Then I started putting some of my stuff up saying it was a collaboration between us. They sold too. He got a posthumous showing at the biggest art gallery in the state and because I told them my pieces and a couple of his were other collaborations, so did I.

I made a mint. Best of all, I said he has hundreds of pieces. He didn't, but since they think my style is his, I can start churning them out. I also saved some of his best work to claim as my own.

The problem is his family is suing me. They had written him off long ago, but now that there's money, they want some. They are even claiming that I've stolen some of his own work and trying to pass it off as my own. Ironically, it's the stuff that's all mine that they're making the claims about, not the stuff that was actually his.

They are even contesting his will just because it wasn't done by a lawyer. I did it the night after he died from a free internet template. The signature is an exact copy, which is to be expected since I became an expert after putting it on so many of my own canvases.

What should I do? Do they have a chance of contesting

the will? And it shouldn't affect the pieces we "did" together, right? And they can't stop me from selling my own artwork just because it looks like what they think is his, can they? I love my new loft on the waterfront and my Jaguar is such a sweet ride I'd hate to have it repossessed. I've enclosed a half dozen original paintings, signed by "us" both to thank you for your help in advance.

  -Artisan in Austin

Dear Artisan,

  Cthulhu would once again like to state he is not an attorney. There are some depths even I will not sink to. However, if the will was not notarized or witnessed by someone other than you, the primary beneficiary, I would think they would have an excellent chance at contesting it. As his next of kin, they would likely be entitled to at least some share of the money from his artistic estate. However, this type of legal infighting can be tied up in the courts for years and years and the first thing their legal representation will likely do is get an injunction against you trying to sell any more of Art's work, which sounds like it would cripple your cash flow unless your work is taking off on its own.

  Cthulhu suggests a peace offering of several dozen pieces. Since you can make more, this shouldn't be an issue. Also, since they live in another city, this would help not to glut your local art market, which would hurt your own sales. In art, there are fads so Art's star will soon fade unless you can produce more footage of him hurting himself artistically. Perhaps digging up his body for a series of viral videos, allegedly set before his demise would help keep your asking prices up, maybe even make them go higher.

I advise this option heartily as Cthulhu now owns originals and I want to make sure I get as much as possible when I sell them. I advise you to be very creative in your productions because I know where you live and I have a high definition camera and Cthulhu is well aware that what would make the paintings even more valuable would be both artists having died in bizarre, but artistic accidents.

Dear Cthulhu,

I am one of the beautiful people. Men want me and women want to be me. Beauty is a burden that I have to bear, but fortunately, it's not that hard. People have always given me stuff and done things for me just because of my looks. It was years before I realized some women actually have to pay for their own drinks in bars. Women are nice to me because they want to be seen with me, especially the less beautiful ones because sometimes a cute guy will pay for their drinks too and sometimes they can pick up my cast-off guys.

All I have to do is bat my eyelashes at a guy to get him to pick up and drop off my laundry, and usually even pay for it. It's a great system except for that one time my silk teddy came back with man goop all over it, but the guy bought me a 54" flat screen TV to apologize, so it worked out okay.

In short, it's my right by beauty to get whatever I want and I like it that way. My problem is with my new job. I graduated college without doing much work other than making sure I had only male or lesbian professors. I sat in the front row in sexy, tastefully revealing outfits, making sure to smile and lean forward every time a professor looked at me. I was rewarded with good grades. True, I could have got a 4.0 if I put out, but I'm no slut. Most of them weren't even worthy to talk to me, let alone touch me. I can't be held responsible if they took my actions and flirting as some sort of insinuation that I might give them a tumble. I mean, all they'd have to do is look at me and then at themselves in a mirror. No one dates that far down. It's hardly my fault Dr. Smith left his wife and six kids for me. He claims he asked me if we could be together if he ditched them, but I don't remember saying yes. True, when people beneath me talk to me and I can't blow them off because

I need something from them, I tend to zone out and just nod a lot and smile. I guess I should have been suspicious when he hugged me and planted a wet one my lips. Not to mention that he rented me an apartment, in which I might add, he thought he was going to live with me after he left his cow of a wife. I told him to get lost and even called the cops, but the apartment was in his name so they said he could stay. I changed the locks when he was out at class and told him to get lost. They evicted me a few weeks later. Turns out the louse only paid the first month's rent.

After graduation, I got hired by this company. I'm not really sure what they do or what my job there is, but they offered me forty grand a year. Chump change I know, but I figured it would build character until I hook some billionaire. By the end of the first week, I had my co-workers fighting for the privilege of doing my work. And by fighting, I mean bare-knuckled boxing in the boiler room. So basically, I come in, sit at my desk, shop on the internet and text my friends all day. It's my kind of position.

That is until my department got a new supervisor. I wasn't worried when I heard his name was Bobby. I figured I'd have him taking me out to lunch by his second day, even if he wasn't straight. Even gay men want to hang out with me too because they want to be me. For the first time ever I was actually wrong.

I knew something was up as soon as I saw "Bobby". It didn't take me long to figure out they only hired him because of some stupid quota. I don't mean he was short or Canadian or something icky like that. It was worse. Bobby was blind. He couldn't see how beautiful I am so he actually expected me to do my own work and when I didn't, he wrote me up. I hadn't finished my probation period, so the company extended it. I hadn't improved by my next review so he told me if I didn't shape up in two weeks, I'd be fired. I said fine, the company could just pay me unemployment. Bobby just laughed. Turns out I hadn't worked there long enough to qualify. So, I got a lawyer who told me my employment was at will or something and I told him I hadn't even met this Will guy, but if he had his number, I was sure I could change his mind. He explained my employer could fire me if they wanted, especially since they were documenting my deficiencies, so I didn't have a case. Worse, he didn't tell me until after I slept with him. Twice. I know I said I wasn't a slut, but I'm not a prude either. This was a partner at one of the biggest law firms in town. The unspoken suggestion that he might get to sleep with me wasn't enough to bend him to my will. I had to put out and dress up like a rodeo clown. It was either that or fork over a five-thousand-dollar retainer. Do you know how many designer outfits that is? Four and a pair of shoes. I wasn't going to let my wardrobe suffer because of Bobby's issues, so I did what I had to do.

I thought about quitting over the principle of it. I could always go back to modeling, but that involved real work, sometimes ten-hour days posing and doing what the photographer tells you, mostly standing or staying still. Besides I tried it for two whole weeks and I didn't get one magazine cover, just page 17 in some swimwear catalog, so I quit.

I figured I needed to get rid of Bobby. I offered the winner of the bare-knuckled boxing tournament a chance to take Bobby out of the picture for me, but it turns out he fell in love with some skank and wasn't interested. He also mentioned some nonsense about killing being morally wrong or something. I can quite remember because I had tuned him out after he said no.

I decided to take matters into my own hands and I pushed Bobby down some stairs. He always worked late. I never did, mainly because they wouldn't pay me for it, but it wasn't hard to hang around. As soon as the clock strikes five, the office clears out faster than a frat party that ran out of beer. I waited quietly at my desk until Bobby walked by a staircase and I pushed him down. I figured I'd get away with it because we were alone and since he was blind, he couldn't identify me.

Well, apparently, the fall didn't kill him. Worse, it seems Bobby has a good sniffer because he was able to identify my perfume. I argued that anyone could be wearing the same perfume, but forgot I had bragged how this chemist I flirted with in college custom made it for me. Turns out he got a job for a perfume company and his stuff sells for a couple hundred an ounce, but he makes this scent only for me. Unfortunately, I may have mentioned that as well.

The police started questioning me and didn't seem to care about how pretty I was. Apparently, both the lobby and the outside of the building I work in have video surveillance and they found footage of me leaving about the time Bobby fell down the stairs. They arrested me and my lawyer won't represent me unless I can come up with the cash since apparently his firm frowns on him sleeping with murder suspects.

Worse, they caught me at the airport and revoked my bail and took my passport, so I'm stuck in jail. I can't afford a decent attorney so I'm stuck with a public defender. He's useless, spending all his time staring at me and trying to look down my orange jumpsuit.

Isn't there some sort of legal defense fund for beautiful people or some sort of amendment in the Declaration of Independence or the Bible to get me out of this? I seem to remember something about all men having the right to be free, so that should doubly apply to a beautiful woman. I'm also worried because I heard that justice is blind so she may feel sorry for Bobby and not give me the get out of jail free card that I'm entitled to. Can you help me and make these people see that what they are doing is wrong? I've enclosed an 8" x 10" glossy of myself, suitable for framing, to help motivate your assistance.

-Beautiful and Entitled In East Encino

Dear Entitled,

Very rarely does Cthulhu get a letter from someone that is more narcissistic than Cthulhu himself, but it does happen. Congratulations on that distinction. As for your problem, first Cthulhu must once again state that humans killing, or trying to kill, other humans is wrong. That task is reserved for Cthulhu alone. Amazingly, it does truly sound like you have managed to get through your existence using nothing more than an accident of birth, probably much like how you came to be in the first place.

Even murderous psychopaths learn that there are consequences for their actions and work to avoid them. Somehow you came to believe you were allowed to act without repercussions based solely on your personal aesthetics. After viewing your photo, I must confess that this alleged attraction escapes me, but most female humans look alike as far as I am concerned. Your physical dimensions are pleasing and enough for a one night stand, however, that is not enough for me to interfere in these matters. That would require a large amount of cash or an actual relationship with Cthulhu. I do not think we would be compatible. A female must care more about Cthulhu than she does herself as well as enjoy long walks on the beach, love kittens (as an appetizer, not the main course), and be extremely fond of tentacles.

Although Cthulhu is not a lawyer, I recommend trying for a plea bargain. Maybe you will get lucky and the DA will be hard up and go along with what you have to offer. I sense your testifying would alienate the jury and have them not only convict you for trying to kill a blind man but also recommending the maximum sentence to the judge.

I would suggest getting your manipulation skills on females fine-tuned. Perhaps you will be able to flirt your way into getting free cigs at the prison commissary, but Cthulhu suspects it will take more than batting your eyelashes. Perhaps find the biggest, toughest woman and attach yourself to her. If media is to be believed, this woman is usually named Bertha and will be going out of her way to meet you regardless. Also, take up a trade because by the time you are paroled, your looks will probably not get you a glass of water.

Dear Cthulhu,

I'm fat and proud of how I got this way. Well, sort of.

It all started when my friend "Guy" and I were goofing around. We started bragging which of us was better than the other. We started talking about the most weight we had ever gained in a short time. Each of us started trying to outdo the other. Before I knew it, Guy had bet me that I couldn't gain 200 pounds in 6 months. Never one to refuse a challenge, especially when drunk, I accepted.

I began to gorge myself. I got season passes to three all you can eat buffets, one each for breakfast, lunch, and dinner. It was tough and as the pounds started to pile on, I even started taking cholesterol medicine to make sure I didn't have a heart attack or stroke.

Six months later when I showed to see if I won, I had to grease the door to get through it. At the weigh in, I tipped the scales. Literally. When I stepped on it, I knocked it over.

Once we righted the scale, I was exactly 200 pounds more than I had been at the start of the bet. My intestines started to rumble. I should have stepped down, but didn't. I let out a fart that lasted over two minutes. The release of gas was so large it caused the scale to drop down to show I had gained only 199.99 pounds.

Now Guy refuses to pay. I think he should because at the start the scale did show 200 and any reasonable person would round the number up for the sake of .01 pounds. Plus, I had to buy an entirely new wardrobe and now I have to pay for massive liposuction to get back to where I was.

Should Guy pay me?

-Gas Attack Victim in Georgia

Dear Gas,

If the bet was for 200 pounds, you lost. Next time, don't use an electronic scale and load up your pockets and bodily orifices with lead weights.

After you go for the liposuction and have your excess adipose sucked out, have your doctor send it to me. I am throwing a dinner party and human fat, mixed with a little garlic and basil, makes a great dip.

Dear Cthulhu,

I'm a ninety-four-year-old man who's been adrift since I lost my wife of sixty-five years. "Trudy" didn't die. She has Alzheimer's and while we were at the mall I lost her. The police have been looking for her for two weeks, but so far nada. I have an etiquette question. How long does she have to be missing before I can start dating again? There's a 76-year-old across the hall at my retirement community who's a real hottie and seems interested.

I figure three weeks tops. What do you think?
-Geezer With A Cane He's Ready To Use

Dear Geezer,

As humans are unable to go without food for three weeks, I would surmise she will have passed by that time, which would release you from your marital vows. Cthulhu would recommend putting up flyers with her picture, maybe offer a reward for the last week so you can be sure she will not show up and ruin your new romance, especially if you had your rendezvous in your apartment and she walked in.

Dear Cthulhu,

I'm a first-time Mom and took my baby out to Chunky Cheddar's Playhouse Restaurant and game room and let her play in the ball pit. I was tired when I took her out. Imagine my shock when I got home and found out the baby I had was a boy. My child was a girl. I had taken the wrong baby. I knew I should have worn my glasses, but I was hoping to hook up with "Josh", the guy who collects the tickets and gives out the prizes and I look hotter without my specs. Besides he had a 1 in 7 chance of being my baby's dad so I wanted to hold her side by side with Josh to see if they looked alike before I sued for child support. Although without my glasses, I still couldn't tell.

Of course, I went back, right after I had dinner and dessert. I asked around and it turns out that no one else had reported a misplaced baby. I spent at least three whole minutes searching the ball pit in case she was still there, but she wasn't. I tried to use my grief to get with Josh, to have him comfort me and all. It didn't pan out because he couldn't take a break, and the manager was yelling at me to watch my kid. I thought about telling him that it wasn't my kid, but I didn't want to get Josh in trouble, so I just went home.

I'm too embarrassed to go to the police. Besides, it's been almost two weeks and that would probably make them ask me even more questions. To tell the truth, I had originally wanted a boy anyway. I figure this was nature's way of giving me what I wanted, which of course is a good thing. Basically, I'm thinking about keeping him. Besides, hospitals switch babies all the time, so what's the big deal, right? I had named my daughter Jan, which can be a boy's or a girl's name. Should I just tell everyone Jan's a boy and when they ask "Wasn't he originally a girl?" just tell them they're nuts?

-Playing Three Card Mommy with Two babies

Dear Three Card,

You humans all look alike to Cthulhu although it is refreshing to find a human who does not get all caught up in the whole parenting thing. You wanted a boy, you got a boy. Move on with your life.

As for Josh, I recommend dropping the child support issue. If he asks for a DNA test, the odds are now much worse than 1 in 7 for him to be the father, unless of course, he spreads his seed around many more times than even you seem to. Also, the same test would prove you are not the mother, which means they may take this child away from you and put you in prison. Or you could shift the blame and sue the hospital, claiming they did it, providing you can convince everyone the gender change was a clerical issue.

Dear Cthulhu,

I have a stuffed version of you. I was wondering what you thought of that and if you got a royalty off of each one?"
-Plush Lover in Laredo

Dear Plush,

Sadly, Cthulhu falls into the celebrity category, which allows people to use my image without having to pay me, much in the same way your Presidents do not get kickbacks from the bobble head dolls fashioned in their image. Like politicians, I get my kickbacks from other areas. And it is said that no publicity is bad publicity.

It also serves another more practical purpose, familiarizing the children with my likeness and greatness, thus helping prepare them for the day I rule over this world and their pathetic lives. Besides, how could anything with my visage not be wonderful?

My only concern with it, and you can be honest with Cthulhu here, is do you think they made me look fat? And my stuffed idol's tentacles seem a little limp, which I assure you mine are anything but.

Dear Cthulhu,

I'm a car lover. Literally. I gain sexual satisfaction from actually having intercourse with automobiles. I trace it back to my youth where the only place I could be alone with my dates was in the backseat of my junker or sometimes their or their parents' cars.

It started insidiously. When I finally had a place of my own, I got busy there, but it just wasn't as good. I started making excuses why my dates couldn't come to my apartment, but after the fifth time in a month I told them it was being fumigated, the ladies started to realize something was wrong. Finally, one of my girlfriends had enough and told me she wasn't a teenager who had to do it in the back of some car and demanded I take her home. I dropped her off, but I was still worked up so I stopped at my favorite lover's lane by my lonesome and climbed in the back seat to take care of business. It was amazing so I started doing it more often. I made modifications to my backseat to make it more, well, accommodating. Besides my hands get tired and I'm just not flexible enough to… well, let's just say I can't do it tongue in cheek and leave it at that.

Around that time, I started finding cars attractive. Especially red sporty ones. The more expensive the hotter I think they are. I started going to lover's lane on foot and getting it on with the cars I found there, especially the ones out of my price range. Since the owners were inside, I had to satisfy myself on the outside, using the tailpipe more often than not. Sadly, I'm not a big enough guy for that to be overly satisfying, plus that part of the car heats up quite a bit, so I invented an insulated doohickey that inserts inside the pipe. It's filled with a thick gel like an ice pack and lubricated. It's really good, especially if the engine is revving at the time. Let me tell you, no woman can do that. I've debated about trying to get it patented, but I haven't yet found a message board or a group of people with like interests, so I'm sure if it'd be worth investing the money.

Problem is, I've been getting noticed. Folks have been calling the cops on me and I've only barely gotten away a couple of times. A few have even taken cell phone pictures and videos of me in the act. Fortunately, I wear a Halloween mask so I'm not recognizable, except for the tattoo on my butt. They've even run edited footage on the local news and let me tell you, it's hot.

Worse, the cops are now staking out the lover's lanes, scaring all the hot cars away. Once I went at one of the cop cars, but they noticed the car rocking and came out after me and I had to leave before I was finished. I hate that. Worse, according to the news reports, they've found DNA evidence at some of my rendezvous, so if they catch me, they'll link me to the crime. I can't do no time. There ain't no cars in jail and I won't do a convict bus. I have my standards.

I'm thinking about seeking out cars like a Lamborghini, a Ferrari and so on, but people don't just park those kinds of rides on the street. I'd have to break into garages, which means worrying about alarms, maybe even some guy with a shotgun looking to protect his vehicle. I've been studying how to break into cars on the Internet and I think I can do it, which would be great. Even thinking about getting in the backseats of those babies makes my knee quiver, especially since I've modified my doohickey to fit in cup holders.

The question is, is it worth the risk? Breaking into a house's garage carries a bigger penalty than just breaking into a car, right? And do you think it's worth patenting my doohickey? I'd love to have my own business, but it has to be something I'm passionate about. And do you think the television station would send me copies of the footage of me and the cars if I called and asked nicely?

-Car Love Machine In Michigan

Dear Car,

Cthulhu is not a lawyer, but someone can shoot you for breaking in his house with limited penalties, so I think you may be right. As for your doohickey sideline, it has been my experience with humans that there is no perversion so depraved that someone won't indulge in. And if the perversion becomes a trend, others will try it out of curiosity, boredom and a misguided desire to fit it. Judging by the Dear Cthulhu mailbag, if you could further expand your modifications to include livestock, I think you could become a rich man.

You are however missing a better business opportunity. Valet parking. Offer high-end restaurants your services, undercutting the competition and you will be able to indulge your fantasies at your leisure without risk of being surprised by a shotgun. Or consider doing the same with car detailing. That would give you even more time along with the objects of your desires. And if you do an exceptional job you should get enough business to keep you busy and satisfied. And a last option, buy or get a job at a long-term parking lot near an airport.

Do not call the television stations. It will only bring attention to yourself and increase your risk of being caught. The smart move is to hope the original filmers put it on I-tube or simply set up your own cameras next time.

Dear Cthulhu,

I'm an EMT. I love my job, but my shift switches every week, so it's difficult for me to get another job and I've been having some money problems. It's not my fault, but lately, I've become addicted to women's panties. No, it's nothing sick or sorted. All I do with them is wear them. It's embarrassing to admit, but I love the way thongs and crotchless panties feel, especially under my uniform. And I hate to confess it, but I don't like wearing a pair more than once. The thrill is gone after the first time. Plus, I'm a big guy and I do stretch them out, so they don't feel the same.

I make decent money, but not enough to induce my high-end tastes for my daily silk fix. Then I realized that I dealt with a lot of people who are lying down with an oxygen mask over their faces or sometimes even unconscious. They have purses and wallets. The first time I lifted a guy's wallet as I was giving him CPR, I felt really bad until the shipment from Vicky's of Hollywood arrived. It became a thrill to get away with the theft. I started going to sporting and concert events just to pickpocket people. It was a rush. I now have enough panties to last me for almost three years, but I can't stop the stealing.

Enough people, at least the ones that survived, have started filing complaints with the hospital and they are investigating the thefts. Sooner or later, they'll realize I was the common factor.

How do I get out of this?

-Cross-dressing Pickpocket in Kansas

Dear Pickpocket,

First, you should at least be smart enough to dispose of the wallets and purses in such a way that they cannot be traced back to you. Also, make sure you vary your disposal method and site or you may find police waiting for you the next time you drop one off.

Since you seem to have an addictive personality and get off on the thrill, I have a solution, at least for work. Take the wallets, empty most of the cash and return the wallet to the patient's pocket. First, by leaving some money you aren't being greedy and stupid. The person might assume they miscounted or lost it somehow. Second, returning the wallet is much more difficult and risky, which should increase your rush.

There is one thought that should comfort you or at least your mother. If you are caught and try to get away in the ambulance and have an accident, at least you'll be wearing clean underwear.

Dear Cthulhu,

I'm a long-time fan, first-time letter writer. Just a quick question. My husband and I are newlyweds and we're having our first dinner party. He says the napkins should be folded as rectangles on the left side of the plate, while I was always taught that they should be triangles. Which way is right? Please help us, because this looks like this could be our first major fight, which would be unfortunate because my hubby is not much of a fighter so I'd clobber him and all those bruises would raise questions I'd rather not have to explain to our guests. Sadly, I always believed in the saying that if someone wasn't a fighter, they were a lover. Hubby stinks in both departments, but that's what I get for saving myself for marriage I guess. I should have gone for a test drive on his love machine and I could be giving this party solo instead of arguing about napkins. Live and learn.

   -Unfolded In Florida

Dear Unfolded,

Napkin folding is a matter of preference and style, although the triangle form is more prevalent. These days many restaurants don't even bother with either, simply choosing to wrap the silverware in the cloth and plopping it on the table. This is a practice I abhor and frankly lowers the amount I tip.

I suggest a compromise. Do a search on the internet for napkin origami and fold all the napkins into the shapes of different animals. I am fond of the duckie myself, but the swan is also nice.

I am sorry about your man trouble. I may be able to help you in that department as well. Simply invite Cthulhu to this dinner party. I can assure you nobody will care about the napkins once I arrive. Cthulhu is very good at party games like charades and Operation, although I will admit the first time I played I did not realize players were supposed to use a plastic board, not the fellow guests. I feel my way takes more skill and is far more enjoyable, but no one seems to want to volunteer to be the patient.

Then after the rest of the guests go home, you and I can retire to the bedroom where I will show you what an unforgettable lover Cthulhu is. We can even let your husband watch in the hopes that he might learn a thing or two. I must warn you, that being with me may ruin you for human males. It is the tentacles that do it. And from past experience, I can say it is likely that your husband may never want to touch you again, but judging by your complaints that does not sound like it would be too great a loss.

I look forward to getting my invitation.

Dear Cthulhu,

I'm worried about my four-year-old daughter. We have two dogs and just got a kitten. Yesterday, we had to leave the house and I couldn't find "Kitty" anywhere. I asked my daughter where she was and she just told me she was hiding. I finally gave up and went to put my coffee cup in the microwave. When I opened the door, I found Kitty. She wasn't moving, so at first, I assumed the worst, but she was just sleeping. When I asked my daughter how the cat got in the microwave, at first she told me she didn't know, but she finally admitted she put her in there because she kept eating the dogs' food and she was helping the dogs.

My husband says I'm blowing this out of proportion because she didn't turn the microwave on, but I'm worried. I've heard stories about serial killers who killed animals as small children and I think my daughter may be going down that road. Part of me doesn't want that, but another part of me already knows she's not going to become a doctor or a lawyer and this would be something that stands out. I'd have stories to tell at the hairdressers and when I'm out at parties. Then there would be media coverage, a possible book and movie deal, so I have to admit part of me is intrigued.

Am I being a bad mother?

-Mother of Catty Daughter in Kansas

Dear Mother,

Yes, you are. Cthulhu sides with your husband on this. The child had no ill will toward the animal and did not harm it. In fact, in her mind, she was helping the other household pets. This shows compassion and even loyalty because she chose to help the animals she has known longer. To her, the microwave was probably a small cubbyhole. However, if your goal is for her to become a serial killer, there is still time. Most serial killers were abused as children and that is what twists them into monsters. However, Cthulhu has two things to say on that. One, humans should not kill humans as that is Cthulhu's right alone. And two, a parent who harms their offspring in any way is not worthy of life. Should you do anything to harm or try to shape your daughter in this way, Cthulhu will hunt you down and feast on your soul. Slowly.

Dear Cthulhu,

My wife is a huge racing fan. She was that way when I married her but lately, things have changed for the worse. She's given herself the nickname "Speedy" and insists me and the kids call her that. She pretends like she can't hear us if we don't. Whenever we go somewhere, Speedy insists on driving. It's not that I mind being chauffeured, it's that she drives like she's on a track. She'll do upward of 80 MPH in a 30 zone. Speedy's been pulled over a dozen times but gets out of a ticket every time because her dad is the chief of police and her mom is a local judge.

I've tried to get her to go for counseling, but that only made it worse because the therapist made her get in touch with her inner driver. Now she will only turn left, which makes getting off a highway dangerous. Forget about local driving—we live in a part of New Jersey where they make you go right to go left. The bottom line is we have 3 kids and I worry about their safety, especially when I go to work and leave them with their mother.

Worse still, she's out in our garage souping up our minivan with nitrous oxide boosters. She bought a racing jumpsuit and a helmet, which she wears when she drives. Speedy painted a number on the sides of our minivan. That would be the least of it if I didn't have to put up with the snickers and rude comments from the neighborhood guys, which wouldn't even have been an issue if she had chosen any other number but 69.

The very worst part of it is she splits up all her errands. Instead of going to the grocery store, hair salon, and auto parts store in one trip, she stops at the house in between each and expects me and the kids to act as her pit crew. The cost of tires in the past week was more than my last paycheck. When I talked to her about it, Speedy told me not to worry, that we'll only have to pay for the tires until she lands a sponsor like

Greatday or Hotrock Tires. Then she hit me with a tire iron when I suggested that since she wasn't a real racer that might not happen and that it wasn't safe to have the kids work on the car. Our three-year-old cut his hand and needed stitches after using the power impact wrench to take off the lug nuts and the eight-year-old went up like a Roman candle after the racing gas can backed up and dosed him and a spark set him on fire. Luckily, I almost instantly doused him with the racing fire extinguisher Speedy keeps near the car, but he still lost all the hair on his arms and both eyebrows.

I'm at my wit's end. If I leave her, her dad will make my life miserable and if I try to get custody of the kids, her mom will make sure whatever judge I get gives them to her. I've thought about cutting her brake lines, but I'm too worried I'll get caught and I couldn't be sure she wouldn't have the kids in the car with her when the brakes fail. What can I do?

-Married To A Racest

Dear Married,

Once again, Cthulhu must state that humans should not kill humans. That pleasure is reserved for Cthulhu alone. I suggest first trying medication. If you can't get a local physician to prescribe for your wife, maybe for you. Many humans seem to care less while on narcotics. There are several internet sites that will help you out, whether you decide to medicate you or your spouse. Of course, you will have to research which medication you feel will work the best and not have bad side effects. Without any medical background, this will be a challenge, dangerous, and also fun.

I also recommend feeding into her psychosis. Find a local stock car race league and have her join. It is possible that racing for real may decrease her desire to pretend to race. And work hard to convince her that driving on the side decreases her potency on race day. Make up quotes to that effect from racers she admires and post them on the web under another name as if they are news, then show them to her as if you found them.

As for protecting your offspring, mention to her that most sponsors follow child labor laws, at least in their factories in the United States, so using child labor will hurt her chances of landing a sponsorship deal. Of course, that will leave you a one-man pit crew. If she stays in the car, use the power tool to make noises and move around like you are really changing the tires after spraying something foamy on her rear-view mirrors so she can't see. Wipe it off only after you are done. This should save your back and your tire bill.

Dear Cthulhu,

I am a 54-year-old divorced man with no kids and I'm obsessed with the Jabaguy card game. It's based on the Japanese anime cartoon where kids train creatures to fight each other. I'm in a dead-end job, but I'm too old to start over. I haven't had a date in years. My only pleasure in life is playing Jabaguy. Sadly, I just can't seem to get anyone my own age interested in playing, and it just can't be done with any sort of satisfaction over the internet, so I have to go to local comic and game stores for tournaments where the only other players are eleven-year-olds.

Apparently, the parents think it's creepy and seem to suspect I'm some sort of sicko. Nothing could be further from the truth. One store just asked me not to come back because the parents were complaining. It doesn't help that I'm so good at it that I almost always win because I look like a bully. That and

I can afford to buy the rare and powerful cards that the kids can't.

I've tried video games, casinos, even poker but nothing fills up the holes in my soul like this game.

What can I do to put the parents at ease?

-Shunned Old Jabaguy In Jamaica

Dear Shunned,

The simple truth of the matter is that what humans believe to be true is more important than what actually is. Just look at what the governments of the world have gotten you to believe over the years—wrestling is real, your water is safe to drink, they are not experimenting on you, and your vote counts, just to name a few.

You need a spin doctor, a professional PR person to help you convince these parents what you want them to believe. Unfortunately, it sounds like this is out of your price range and you do not appear bright enough to do it on your own.

Your best bet is to give yourself a reason to be there besides the actual playing of the game. Talk to the owners of these stores and see if they will hire you part time to run these tournaments. Offer to teach classes in game strategy at the store and you can play as part of your classes. And stop entering and winning the tournaments. Take a dive and throw a game once in a while because beating an eleven-year-old at a kids' game comes off as mean and immature and the parents on some level probably feel protective and angry that you have taken a victory away from their offspring. Otherwise, you have no chance of winning them over.

And as an added bonus you may qualify for employee discounts on your Jabaguy purchases.

Dear Cthulhu,

I keep having this recurrent dream that I'm in an earthquake and the ceiling over my bed is falling down on me. The quake is unusual in that it is more of a thumping than a shaking and the rhythm varies from slow to frantically fast, then stops.

I thought it was just a dream until a piece of my ceiling fell down and hit me in the head last week. Then last night my ceiling light fixture fell and smashed all over my bedroom floor. I've checked the Internet and there are no reports of any earthquakes in my area. I've asked around, including my upstairs neighbors, a pair of newlyweds, but nobody else has noticed it. Although the newlyweds giggled when they answered.

Is it possible for a quake to be localized to one apartment? Or do you think maybe I have a ghost or poltergeist or something because sometimes I do hear odd moaning.

-Clueless Earthquaker in Oakland

Dear Clueless,

No, earthquakes are larger in scale than a single apartment. Cthulhu is going to go out on a limb (of which I have plenty) to guess that you do not date much. Here is my suggestion. When you are next woken by the thumping and shaking, no matter what time it is, run upstairs to your neighbors and knock on their door. Keep it up until they answer and the quake will magically stop. Continue this until the quakes end or you figure out their source.

Dear Cthulhu,

I am the managing editor of the online speculative fiction magazine Abyss & Apex. I've been a fan of your advice column for some time and would like to extend an offer to you to write a guest editorial in the form of a typical column. I have many questions for you, great one. Are you interested in sharing your wisdom with our readers? We would, of course, pay you for your time.

-Enticing Editor of Electronic Eloquence

Dear Cthulhu,

Dear Cthulhu is always willing to share his wisdom with those less fortunate, which I'm sure covers most of your readership and humanity. A simple delivery of a living human sacrifice or two would suffice.

Dear Cthulhu,

Sadly, we draw the line at killing a human sacrifice. Would cash suffice?

-Enticing Editor of Electronic Eloquence

Dear Enticing,

It will have to do. Even Cthulhu has bills to pay. The monthly dry cleaning for my acolytes alone is enough to lease a new car. Blood is so hard to get out of cotton. Not to mention my supply of tentacle moisturizer. Chapped tentacles aren't pretty and make me cranky.

And Cthulhu would once again like to point out that people should not kill people. That right lies squarely with Cthulhu and his designated representatives. Delivery of said sacrifices, however, is acceptable should you change your mind.

So, send your questions Cthulhu's way and they shall be answered.

Dear Cthulhu,

My thanks. My first question is one that is near and dear to my heart for obvious reasons—What is the fate of short fiction online?

-Enticing Editor of Electronic Eloquence

Dear Enticing,

Short fiction online shall endure for as long as the Internet does. However, the quality shall continue to vary from the brilliant to the trite, from inspiring to repulsive. Not everyone will be as brilliant as Dear Cthulhu, but one can hardly expect that to be the case.

One limitation is, of course, financial, both for the publishers and authors. The sad state of fiction is that it is a labor of love for most of the creative people involved, but bandwidth and hosting must be paid for. Most authors support their craft with day jobs or understanding spouses. Why even Cthulhu himself does not make enough off this column to allow him to live in the lifestyle he has become accustomed to. Luckily, I have my cult to fall back on. The tax breaks alone on running a church are worth their weight in gold. My wealthier worshippers have no problem tithing large portions of their income and the poorer ones are always willing to sell flowers at the airport, bootlegged DVD's on the street, Amway door to door and the occasional organ when times are tight or I am feeling peckish.

The reader, of course, can help by supporting their favorite sources of fiction anyway they can. Subscribe. Hit the Paypal button and donate a dollar or two or ten. If there are banner ads, click on them. All of them. You do not even have to look at them. Open them in a new window then close it. The site still gets credit for the click. Tell your friends. Mention it on your blog or post it on a message board.

And since it is often a labor of love, the editors and writers involved must have motivation to carry on. They sometimes will get discouraged and will need to feel the love they are laboring for. So, if you read a story you like, drop the author a quick note to tell him or her via the editor. Love the entire issue? E-mail the editor. This makes them know that others appreciate their efforts and will inspire them to carry on And of course, give your utmost support to those who carry Dear Cthulhu, for they are obviously far superior to the rest.

Dear Cthulhu,

Normally at A&A we try to steer clear of endorsing one politician over another, but I understand there is a movement to vote for you in the next presidential election. Why should we vote for you over the other candidates?

-Enticing Editor of Electronic Eloquence

Dear Enticing,

Why one would vote for me over any other should be obvious. As those running this campaign state, why should people have to vote for the lesser of two evils?

However, Cthulhu would like to take this opportunity to state that while I appreciate the movement to have me run for president, I have never actually sought the nomination. The politicians who win are actually responsible to various secret societies and corporations and in theory the voters or computer hackers who put them in office. Cthulhu is responsible to no one and in fact, many of those secret societies and politicians are secretly trying to curry my favor. Ancient evil should not lower itself to enter the fray. That is what lackeys are for. Cthulhu just does not know what Cheney was thinking. Perhaps he was bored.

My only regret is that Obama Girl made the mistake of producing her video for another instead of for Cthulhu. Still, she or any other incredibly hot woman can rectify that oversight and make a Cthulhu Girl (or Cthulhu Girls—Cthulhu is nothing if not a visionary) video. E-mail me and I will even consider a cameo.

Have a Dark Day.

PATRICK THOMAS is the award-winning author of almost 40 books including the beloved fantasy humor Murphy's Lore series, which includes *Tales From Bulfinche's Pub, Fools' Day, Through The Drinking Glass, Shadow Of The Wolf, Redemption Road, Bartender Of The Gods, Nightcaps, Empty Graves, The Mug Life* — as well as the future space adventures *Startenders* and *Constellation Prize*.

The Murphy's Lore After Hours spin-offs star the half pixie/ogre Terrorbelle (*Fairy With A Gun, Fairy Rides The Lightning* and *Terrorbelle The Unconquered*); the former demon-possessed serial killer Agent Karver of the Department of Mystic Affairs *(Dead To Rites, Rites of Passage)*; the cursed magi Hex *(By Darkness Cursed and By Invocation Only)*; Vince Argus, the Soul For Hire *(Greatest Hits)*; and Negral, a forgotten Sumerian god who works as Hell's Detective (*Lore & Dysorder* and *Bullets & Brimstone*).

Co-Written with John French and Diane Raetz, his Mystic Investigators paranormal mystery series includes *Mean Streets* and the omnibus editions *Shadows & Bullets & Brimstone* and *Once Upon In Crime. Assassin's Ball*, his first mystery, is also co-written with John French.

His works include the steampunk *As The Gears Turn* and the space epic *Exile & Entrance*. He co-edited *New Blood* and *Hear Them Roar* and was an editor for the magazines *Fantastic Stories of the Imagination* and *Pirate Writings*.

Patrick's darkly humorous advice column Dear Cthulhu has been running since 2005 and includes the collections *Have A Dark Day, Good Advice For Bad People, Cthulhu Knows Best, Cthulhu Happens, Cthulhu Explains It All* and *What Would Cthulhu Do?* Dear Cthulhu appears monthy on the radio show *Destinies: The Voice of Science Fiction* which is hosted by Dr. Howard Margolin.

His short stories have been featured in over sixty anthologies and more than forty-five print magazines.

A number of his books were part of the props department of the CSI television show and Nightcaps was even thrown at a suspect's head. His urban fantasy Fairy With A Gun had been optioned for film and TV by Laurence Fishburne's Cinema Gypsy Productions. Top Men Productions has turned his Soul For Hire Story, *Act of Contrition*, into a short film.

Please drop by www.patthomas.net or follow him at I_PatrickThomas at Twitter or www.facebook.com/PatrickThomasAuthor to learn more.

More GREAT Science Fiction!

THE STARSCAPE PROJECT

As his quest begins, an artificial intelligence life form enters the galaxy and launches a series covert attacks against the Empire. The Teconeans assume that the Federation is responsible, and galactic peace is about to unravel. As Stryker chases his nemesis into Teconean space, he finds himself thrown into middle of the battle. Knowing that Earth will be the aliens' next target, Stryker must decide whether to let them destroy the Empire, or to forces with his Teconean enemies against the invaders. The key to the mysterious aliens lies buried on the moon of Kennedy Prime, and it's up to Stryker to solve the puzzle before war begins. The fate of the galaxy is at stake.

ZONE OF THE TENTH DGREE

1912, an alien ship crash lands in the Atlantic ean, setting up a secret colony that remains detected for centuries, allowing them to nipulate some of the most important events in man history -- from the sinking of the Titanic to Bermuda triangle to global warming. Now, technology of the 26th century has covered the aliens' distress beacon, and it's a e against time as the Navy tries to stop a rorist armed with a nuclear weapon from stroying the colony and triggering an all-out r as the mother-ship approaches

Now available from

One Last Chance to Save Happily Ever After

Can a group of heroes including Goldenhair, Red Riding Hood and Rapunzel help General Snow White and her dwarven resistance fighters defeat the tyrannical Queen Cinderella? And will they succeed before a war with Wonderland destroys everything?

Their only hope to stop Cinderella's quest for power lies with a young girl named Patience Muffet who carries the fabled shards of Cinderella's glass slippers.

Roy Mauritsen's fantasy adventure fairy tale epic begins with *Shards Of The Glass Slipper: Queen Cinder.*

"Fantastic... A Magnificent Epic!"
-*Sarah Beth Durst* author of *Into The Wild & Drink, Slay, Love*

"The Brothers Grimm meets Lord Of The Rings!"
-*Patrick Thomas,* author of the *Murphy's Lore* series

"Shards is a dark, lush, full-throttle fantasy epic that presents a bold re-imagining of classic characters."
-David Wade, creator of 319 Dark Street

"Roy Mauritsen's enchanting epic comes at a time when fairy tales are back in the forefront of our collective imagination."
-Darin Kennedy, short fiction author

PADWOLF PUBLISHING

In paperback & e-book
Find out more at:
shardsoftheglassslipper.com
padwolf.com

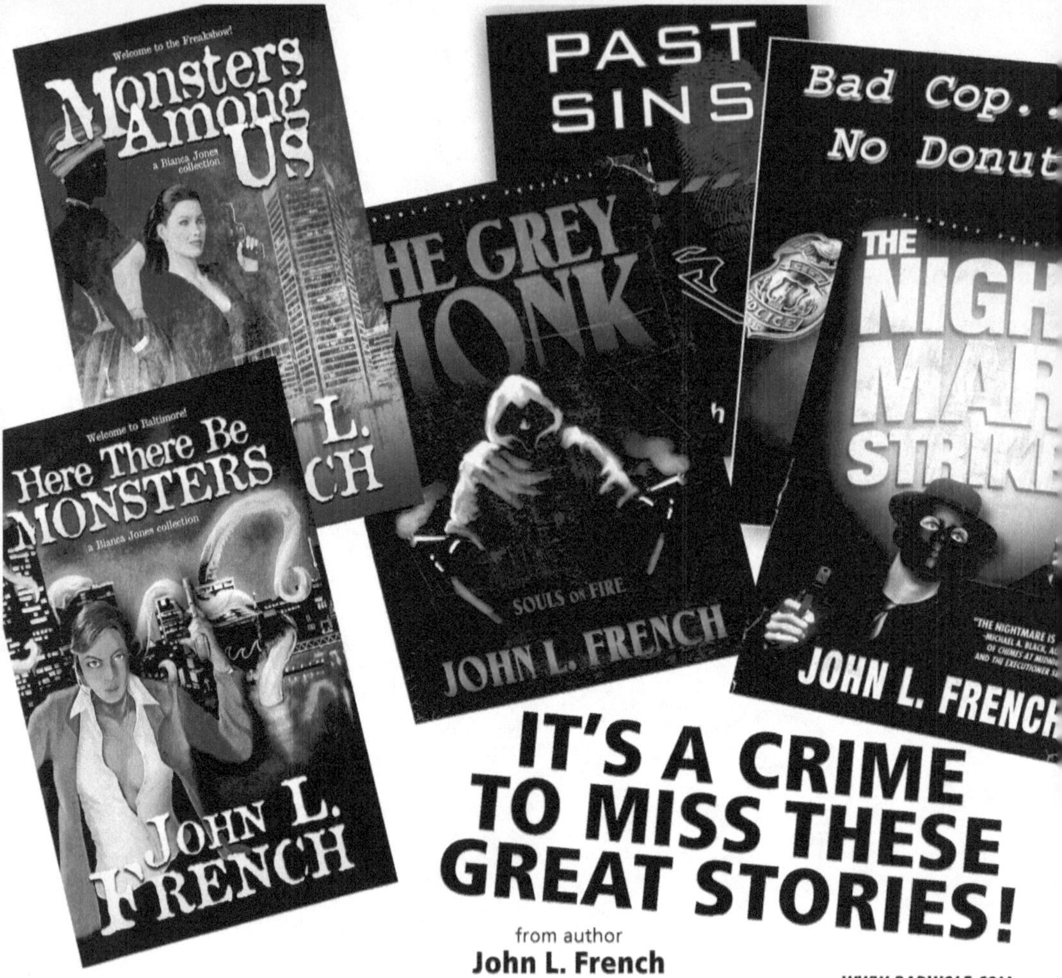

DOWN THESE
MEANS STREETS
of Magic & Monsters walk the

MYSTIC INVESTIGATORS